THE COMPUTE

Also by Elizabeth Levy and available in Target:

Dracula is a Pain in the Neck
Frankenstein Moved in on the Fourth Floor

THE COMPUTER THAT SAID STEAL ME

Elizabeth Levy

TARGET

A TARGET BOOK
published by
the Paperback Division of
W.H. ALLEN & Co. PLC

A Target Book
Published in 1986
by the Paperback Division of
W.H. Allen & Co. PLC
44 Hill Street, London W1X 8LB

First published in the United States of America by
Four Winds Press, 1983

Copyright © Elizabeth Levy, 1983

Printed and bound in Great Britain by
Anchor Brendon Ltd, Tiptree, Essex

ISBN 0 426 20246 5

This book is sold subject to the condition that
it shall not, by way of trade or otherwise,
be lent, re-sold, hired out or otherwise circulated
without the publisher's prior consent in
any form of binding or cover other than that in
which it is published and without a similar
condition including this condition being imposed
on the subsequent purchaser.

CONTENTS

CHAPTER 1

THERE'S NO LUCK
IN CHESS

Adam moved in for the kill. He could feel Tracey's fear, and it made his own heart pound. Tracey's eyes flicked up to the two boys and one girl standing over her. Their eyes refused to meet hers.

Adam knew that Tracey hated to be humiliated, but she had made a mistake in her opening move, and she was trapped.

'Stop smiling to yourself,' Tracey complained to Adam. She twirled a lock of her long dark hair around her forefinger, a nervous habit. She picked up the black knight that Adam knew he had to sacrifice.

Adam tried to keep from smiling, but he loved to win. Tracey was the only one in the sixth grade who could give him a challenge. When they played chess, they were enemies. When they weren't playing chess, they were close friends. When they played Dungeons and Dragons, Tracey and Adam were often co-Dungeon Masters. They could work together for hours setting up scenarios for their friends. When they were characters in a Dungeons and Dragons game, Tracey and Adam saved each other's lives so often that other Dungeon Masters complained. Yet when they played chess against each other, they played to win.

Adam picked up his bishop. Tracey cursed. She saw where he was going, and she knew it was all over. She twisted her neck to relieve the tension and stood up. The Math-Science Club was located in the basement of the school. The only thing in the room that didn't look like it was bought at a tag sale from a police station was a dusty green velvet couch, donated by Tracey's mother.

'Is Adam getting lucky again?' asked Jesse, one of the club members watching the game.

'There's no luck in chess,' Tracey muttered. 'You know that.'

'Tracey was right,' thought Adam. When you lost at chess, you always knew you had made a mistake. Adam's father called chess the most depressing game in the world. He hated chess and couldn't believe it when Adam had begun to play with his grandfather when Adam was only eight. Even as a toddler, Adam had loved the feel of chess pieces in his hand.

His grandfather taught him that in chess you have to look for your opponent's weakness. 'Crush their egos,' said his grandfather. 'Bobby Fisher says that's why he loved to play.'

Tracey moved her queen halfway out onto the board and swept Adam's bishop into her hand. Adam swallowed hard. He hadn't seen that move coming. At first he thought she was a fool, leaving her queen out in the open, but as he studied the board he realised that there was no way he could get at her. With the next move, she would have his king trapped.

Tracey met his eyes. She looked triumphant. Adam saw there was no escape.

'There's no luck in chess,' Adam repeated, 'just skill and strategy.'

Tracey crossed her arms over her chest. She grinned. 'My chess computer pulled that move on me this weekend,' she said happily. 'I was just waiting for a chance to use it on you.'

'Wonderful,' moaned Adam. 'I'm glad I gave you the opportunity.'

Tracey stood up. She was just as tall as Adam and just as skinny. She certainly didn't look like a brain. She was the best-looking girl in the Math-Science Club, and Adam thought she had been elected president half on her looks.

Tracey stuck out her hand. 'That's the second time I've beaten you in a month,' she crowed. 'It's because I'm playing with my chess computer. You ought to get one.'

Adam laughed to himself. He wondered if Tracey thought everyone was as rich as she.

'Do you want to come over to my house and play on my chess computer tonight?' Tracey asked.

'I've got to baby-sit for Alison tonight,' said Adam. 'Mom and Dad have a meeting.'

Adam looked at his watch. 4:44. His parents would be waiting to drive him home. He gathered up his books and homework assignments.

'I'll walk up with you,' said Tracey. 'I have to get home, too.' Tracey lived in a mansion on Middlesex Road, only a few doors from the school. 'Middlesex' was always good for a joke. Tracey had to endure a lot of jokes about it. But Adam didn't tease her about the street's name. He was in awe of the size of her house. It looked almost as big and fancy as their school.

St Luke's, the private school where Adam's parents both worked, and Tracey and Adam were students, had been an all-boys' private school until the late 1970s.

Adam received a full scholarship to St Luke's because his father taught first grade and his mother was the librarian in the primary school. They had moved to Buffalo last year when Adam's father lost his job teaching at a public school in California because of tax cuts.

Adam's father was born in Buffalo, but he had left for California when he was eighteen. Adam would never forget the months that his father agonised over whether or not to go 'home' again. But St Luke's was one of the few schools that had offered his parents a job. His father didn't

9

like being back, but Adam loved Buffalo.

They lived in a much nicer home than the tiny apartment they had in San Francisco. He liked the fact that it felt safe to walk in their neighbourhood, and he liked the kids in Buffalo. Even the richest ones like Tracey weren't snobby or into liquor or pot the way even some of the fourth graders had been in California.

Adam's parents were waiting for him in the Great Hall, an oak-panelled lobby with Gothic arches. His mother wore her hair long. It almost reached her waist. It was silky and straight, the colour of dark, polished wood. Many kids, including Tracey, told Adam they thought his mother was beautiful. Adam thought so, too, but often he wished she would cut her hair. It took hours to dry, and sometimes she said she couldn't go out because her hair was drying.

'Hi, Tracey,' said Adam's father. 'Who won your chess game today? Whoops, never mind. I can tell from Adam's expression, you did.'

Tracey laughed. Tracey had told Adam his father had been voted the cutest teacher in the school. 'I wish he had been my teacher in the first grade,' said Tracey. 'Everybody loves his curly beard.'

Adam didn't know how he felt about having a father whom everyone called cute. All he knew was that he couldn't wait to graduate into the high school so that at least he'd be in a separate building from his parents.

CHAPTER 2

BLUE MEANIES/ BABY-SITTING BLUES

'Do you know *why* Tracey beat me?' Adam asked at dinner that night.

'Is this a riddle?' asked Adam's mother, trying to get Adam's two-year-old baby sister, Alison, to stop throwing peas on the floor.

'No. It's not a riddle. I used to *always* beat Tracey, but now she has a chess computer and she's getting better than me.'

Adam's father laughed. 'Now, that's got to be a new excuse.'

'Don't laugh,' said Adam, but found himself laughing anyhow. It did sound pretty silly blaming the chess computer for his loss.

'What's a chess computer?' asked Adam's mother.

'It's neat,' said Adam. 'It's an electronic game designed by great chess masters. You can play at all different levels. My game would really get better if I had one.'

'One more gadget,' said Adam's father. 'Everyone thinks his or her life will get better with just one more gadget.'

'Come on, Dad. That's not fair. You don't even play chess, so of course you wouldn't want one.'

'You're right, but I bet I wouldn't want one even if I did

play chess.'

'But that doesn't mean *I* can't want one.'

'You can want one,' said Adam's father. 'But we can't afford one.'

He had a chuckle in his voice, and Adam knew his father was trying to keep the conversation light, but Adam wasn't joking. He really did want a chess computer. It *would* improve his game.

'If you paid me for baby-sitting, then I'd buy it myself,' said Adam.

Adam's mother frowned. 'We've been through that before,' she said. 'You know I don't believe in that. We're a family. We help each other. Dad and I don't charge you for meals. This family isn't run on the exchange system. We all pull together.'

'Besides,' added Adam's father, ' we can't afford the prices kids get for baby-sitting these days.'

'But it's not fair,' complained Adam. 'If I baby-sat for someone else, I'd get paid.'

'We're not "someone else." We're your family.'

'We are family!' Adam's father started to sing the old disco song. 'Mama, papa, baby, and me . . .' Alison banged her spoon in rhythm.

'See, we've got our own rhythm section,' said Adam's father. 'And Alison isn't asking to be paid.'

'I still say it's not fair,' said Adam.

'That's what John F. Kennedy said, and he got to be president,' teased Adam's father. 'Maybe you'll be president someday.'

'He said it when he was president,' snapped Adam's mother. 'And it was a callous thing to say anyhow.'

'Hey, wait a minute,' said Adam's father quickly. 'This is a family that pulls together, remember? There's no need to snap at me.'

Adam played with the food on his plate.

Adam's mother stood up and helped Alison out of her high chair. 'We'd better be going. We'll be late.'

'What meeting do you have tonight?' Adam asked.

Adam's mother sighed. Then she smiled. 'It must seem to you that we've got nothing but meetings, doesn't it? Either we've got school meetings ... or ...'

'This is a meeting about the nuclear freeze movement,' said Adam's father. 'You know, disarmament ... make the world safe for all you kids ...'

'Gee, thanks, Dad,' said Adam sarcastically.

Adam's father winked at him. 'Well, we don't want you to go up in smoke,' he said. 'Or would you rather die young with a chess computer in your arms?'

'I don't see why I have to make a choice,' said Adam.

'You always were the logical one,' said Adam's father. He bent over to kiss him lightly on the top of his head. 'We should be home by ten.' He picked Alison up and held her tightly. 'Be a good girl and don't give Adam any trouble.'

Adam's mother gave them both a kiss. 'On the refrigerator I left the number where we'll be.' She gave Adam a hug. 'Thanks for taking care of Alison for us.'

Adam took Alison to the front window so she could watch the car leave. He looked out at the snow, shining under the streetlights. The new snow was like a glitter dust over the dirty white piles underneath. Adam loved to watch the drifts in front of his house grow. Tracey was a native Buffalonian, and she told him that two-foot snowdrifts were nothing. But San Francisco almost never got snow, and Adam loved the snow.

Adam got so lost in watching the snow that he forgot about Alison. He turned around and saw her toddling toward him, holding on to a magic marker pen as if it were the only thing keeping her upright. The top of the pen was off, and her face was covered with blue marks, as if she were dressed up to audition to be a rock star.

Adam turned his full attention to Alison. 'Give me the pen,' he said. Alison hugged the pen closer, putting a dark splotch on her turtleneck, already grubby with leftover food from dinner.

'*My pen!*' Alison shouted.

'I know, but if you give it to me, we can draw a picture

together.'

'Draw blue meanie,' Alison demanded.

Adam smiled. Alison loved 'The Yellow Submarine.'
'Okay,' he said. 'Wait while I put on the music.'

He put on the Beatles. Alison handed him the pen and
wiggled up on the couch next to him. 'When the music's
over, Alison goes to bed, okay?' Adam said hopefully.

The phone rang. Adam leaned over Alison to pick it up.
It was Jesse Stone. 'Hiya, Adam, what's going on? It
sounds like a party.'

Jesse was one of Adam's closest friends, but he always
acted a little hurt, as if Tracey and Adam were deliberately
leaving him out of things. Yet, they didn't. Jesse was a
charter member of the Math-Science Club and of their
Dungeons and Dragons game. Adam liked Jesse. It wasn't
just that Jesse was smart, he was funny, too. But Adam
wished that he didn't always sound so hurt.

'It's not a party,' said Adam. 'I'm baby-sitting.'

'Pretty plushy to be paid for staying home on a snowy
night.' Jesse was an only child.

'I'm not paid,' said Adam, catching the phone with his
chin so that he could keep his hand free to finish his
drawing for Alison. Alison sensed she wasn't getting his
full attention. She started to crawl off the couch.

'I have something important to talk about. I want to
change our Dungeons and Dragons game on Saturday. My
mom says that the skiing will be terrific. She's willing to
take us all. Want to come?'

Adam hesitated. All fall they had played Dungeons and
Dragons on Saturday, and Adam preferred Dungeons and
Dragons to skiing. He had only been skiing a few times,
and he wasn't very good at it. Neither of his parents skied,
so he only went when Tracey or Jesse invited him.

'I don't know,' said Adam hesitantly. 'I'd hate to give up
Dungeons and Dragons all winter.'

'Who said anything about giving it up?' asked Jesse,
half laughing. 'Why not have both? We can go skiing and
then come back here for dinner. We'll play afterwards.

You can even spend the night.'

'Well, check with Tracey and see if she wants to go skiing,' said Adam.

'I did. Of course, she wants to go skiing.'

Adam swallowed. He didn't know why it bothered him that Jesse had called Tracey first. 'Okay,' he said, looking around the living room and realising that Alison had disappeared. 'Look, I've got to find my sister. She's probably getting into trouble somewhere.'

'Well, I wanted to talk to you about the math homework,' said Jesse, sounding as if he thought Adam was making up an excuse to get off the phone.

'I'll try to call you after she goes to sleep,' said Adam. He hung up the phone quickly.

The house was silent. 'Alison!' shouted Adam, worried because she was being so quiet.

'Alison!' he shouted more sharply.

The snow muffled the sounds from the street. Adam checked to make sure the door to the basement was closed. Once he had left it open, and Alison had tumbled down, luckily landing on a pile of laundry on the bottom of the steps.

The only sound that Adam could hear was the hiss of the radiator. Adam looked at the front door. Alison was just tall enough to reach the doorknob, standing on tiptoes. Had she managed to go out in the freezing cold? Adam could just see her frozen to death by a kerb down the block. He wondered how long it would take a two-year-old kid to freeze.

'*Alison! Answer me!*' he shouted, but the only answering sound was the stupid hiss of the radiator.

Adam raced up the stairs, trying to remember if he had drained the tub after giving Alison her bath. Could she have crawled into the tub and drowned? He imagined himself having to call his parents and tell them.

He looked in the bathtub. It was empty. Her rubber frog lay on his back near the drain.

'*Alison!*' he shouted again. He peered into her room.

The light was out, but there was a bump in her crib, and a chair was pulled next to it.

He flicked on the light. Alison peeked out at him, two small eyes among all the glass ones of her stuffed animals.

'What the hell are you doing in there?' he asked.

'Bad word,' said Alison.

Adam cursed to himself. 'Why didn't you answer when I called?' he asked.

'Adam said go sleep after music,' said Alison sweetly, hugging her unicorn.

'How did you get in here?' asked Adam. 'I didn't know you could get into your crib yourself.'

'Chair,' said Alison smugly. Adam knew she thought she had pulled off a great joke by hiding in her own crib, and he had to admit that she had.

'Okay, now that you're in here, stay,' he said. 'Is your diaper wet?'

Alison shook her head. Adam tried to feel underneath to see if she was lying.

'*No! No!*' screamed Alison.

Adam sighed. 'Okay ...' He figured that if she wet in her sleep, she'd be no more wet than she was now, and maybe she was telling the truth.

'Good night, Alison.' He leaned over the crib and kissed her on top of her head. Her silky hair felt soft to his lips.

He tiptoed out of the room and went back down to the living room to get out his homework. When his parents were out, he liked to work in there with the stereo on. He flipped over the Beatles record.

'*Mommy!*' screamed Alison at the top of her lungs. Adam headed up the stairs, taking them two at a time. She sounded as if she were being attacked.

He went into her room. Alison was standing up in her crib, shaking it furiously.

'Where Mommy?' she screamed.

'Alison, Mommy went out. You know that. But I'm here.'

'Mommy! Mommy!' she screamed. Two fat tears fell

from the corner of her eyes. She looked like an orphan on the television news.

Adam picked her up and held her against his chest. 'Alison, Mommy and Daddy will be back soon, but you have to be a good girl and go to sleep.'

Alison gave him a look of total trust, as if she completely understood. She burped. Adam lay her back down and rubbed her back. He knew she liked that.

'I love you, Adam,' Alison said in a voice perfectly clear, with no hint of baby talk.

'I love you, too ... now go to sleep,' said Adam.

He tiptoed out again.

He put the record player back on very low, wishing that he had a Walkman. Maybe he could convince his parents that it would be a good investment because then he could listen to music without waking up Alison.

Adam had to write a theme on humour and the Greek gods. He thought about Hermes who drove his older brother, Apollo, crazy. Everybody thought Hermes was so clever in stealing Apollo's cows, and always getting Apollo in trouble, but Adam thought he would write about Hermes from Apollo's point of view.

Adam glanced around the living room full of books, so much smaller than the rooms of most of his friends. But his mother kept their shelves as well organised as the library's. He knew right where to find the books on the Greek gods.

CHAPTER 3

THE FASTER YOU GO, THE HARDER YOU FALL

Adam wished Tracey would stop talking. The chair lift was coming closer, and he turned to watch it. Tracey slipped into the chair as naturally as if the chair weren't moving at all, but Adam had to concentrate with all his might. To him, getting on the chair was the scariest part about skiing. The chair seemed to be moving so slowly. Then suddenly it was there, bumping into the small of his back, and he had to jump on.

Adam's mittened hand gripped the aluminium side of the chair. Now was the worst moment, hanging in space, feeling as if he would pitch forward before he could get the safety bar down. Tracey twisted in the chair, totally without fear, and brought the safety bar down in front of them.

Adam kept his hand gripped to the side. Tracey settled back. 'Relax,' she said. 'Are you this uptight on airplanes, too?'

'No,' said Adam. 'On airplanes I feel perfectly safe. If anything happens to me on an airplane, it's not my fault. I can't fall out of an airplane because I'm a klutz.'

'But you don't feel safe now?' Tracey asked.

Adam swallowed hard. The chair jerked as it went

through the rollers connected to the poles. 'No.'

Tracey laughed. She leaned over the safety bar and watched the skiers beneath her. *'Hey! Daniel, you hotshot!'* she shouted at her brother. Tracey twisted around in the chair to watch her brother continue down the slope.

'Tracey, would you mind not jumping around,' said Adam. 'This chair is swinging so much it might come off its cable.'

'Honest, Adam, you act like a little old man. I wish you'd relax.'

'I was born relaxed. In fact, my father says that at my delivery I came into the world like I was getting out of a warm bath. He says Alison came into the world like a live wire, ready for action.'

'Well, I think he's nut, or else you've changed. You're not at all relaxed. You could win an award for the most unrelaxed kid in the sixth grade.'

Adam wondered about what Tracey said. His parents thought of him as relaxed. 'Adam never gives us any trouble.' Adam always felt somewhat condemned. As if he entered the world *too* relaxed. He could remember his parents telling him that when he was a baby, sometimes they would sneak into his room just to make sure he was still breathing. 'You were such a quiet baby.'

'Better wake up,' said Tracey. 'We're almost at the top.' Adam hated getting off the chair lift only a little less than he hated getting on. Tracey lifted the safety bar and sailed off. Adam followed her, ducking so that the chair lift would miss him. He did a perfect snowplough down the little hump of snow that led off the chair.

Tracey waited for him, adjusting her ski poles. 'Ready?' she said.

'Shouldn't we wait for Jesse and his mom?'

Tracey made a face. 'They're so slow!'

'So am I!'

'Yeah, but you at least try. Jesse just complains. You only complain about going up. You don't complain about the good parts.'

Adam grinned. Tracey made him feel terrific. It was true, Adam was afraid of the chair, but he wasn't afraid of going fast. He pushed off, following Tracey. Her skis were almost perfectly parallel. She attacked the moguls like her brother. Adam crossed the slope, making wide turns. He wasn't embarrassed to snowplow when he had to, but he managed to keep Tracey in sight. He loved the feel of going fast, the clatter of his skis on the icy patches. When he went fast, there was no time to think, no time to figure out what moves to make. His body made the moves without his mind, and he loved that feeling.

Tracey waited for him halfway down the slope. 'You're looking good, especially for a beginner. Try pushing off from the moguls though. You just sort of hump over them. If you use them to make your turns on the top of them, you won't look so jerky.'

'If I'm looking good, how come I look jerky?'

Tracey shrugged. 'You're a good-looking jerk, okay?'

'Who needs you?' said Adam, pushing off, but as he went over the next mogul, he bent his knees and pushed around the mound of snow. He slid down the other side, gathering speed.

'Excellent!' yelled Tracey behind him.

Adam could feel his skis getting ahead of him, going a little too fast. He struggled to keep his weight forward, but his skis moved faster than he did. He felt himself falling over backward, landing on his back. He rolled down the hill, snow filling his mouth and caking his eyes. He tried to stop himself, but gravity was pulling him faster and faster. He hit some ice and he couldn't get his edges to connect with anything so that he would stop. He felt the safety release on his ski give.

Finally he came to a stop. He put his mittened hand to his face. It felt as if his eyebrows were crusted over with two inches of snow. His cheeks stung as if they had been scraped with number 10 sandpaper.

Tracey swooped to a perfect stop in front of him. 'Are

you okay?'

Adam caught his breath. 'Yeah, I just think I swallowed half the slope.' He tried to stand up, but his skis slipped out from under him. He slid three more feet down the slope. Tracey anchored herself in front of him, using her weight to hold his skis until he could stand up.

Adam shook the snow off his parka and hat. His left leg was shaking – as if it had a life of its own. 'I just learned a lesson in aerodynamics. The faster you go, the harder you fall,' he said.

Adam heard the clatter of skis behind him. 'Wow! That was some fall!' Jesse skidded to a stop. 'Are you okay?'

'I'm fine,' said Adam, looking up the slope to where he began his fall. He must have slipped over a hundred yards.

'Adam, are you all right?' asked Jesse's mother. She was a tall, blond woman who was an excellent skier.

'I'm fine,' said Adam. 'I think it looked worse than it was.'

'Well, I'm glad we caught up with you. We'd better make this our last run. It's almost four.'

'Oh, please, Margaret, can't we have one last run?' pleaded Tracey. 'We'll make it fast.'

'Not today. Adam has to return his skis and I have to get back to town.'

Secretly Adam was pleased that the day was over. Another go up the chair lift didn't appeal to him.

'Come on, kids, I'll race you down.' Jesse's mother dipped her skis straight down.

'Some race,' muttered Adam, watching her glide up and down over the moguls, her strong legs pushing her closer and closer to the fall line, the imaginary straight line that runs straight up and down the mountain.

'Your mom sure is a beautiful skier,' Adam said to Jesse.

'She was on her ski team in college.'

'I wish my parents skied,' said Adam.

'Why are we wasting time talking?' asked Tracey. 'Let's go. She said it was a race.'

'A race she knew she'd win,' grumbled Jesse, but he

21

followed Tracey. Technically, Jesse was a much better skier than Adam. He made perfectly controlled parallel turns. Adam watched his two friends ahead of him. They were both so lucky, and they didn't even realise it. They owned their own skis. They didn't have to rent battered old skis. They had so much, they never even thought about money. They went skiing in the winter, away to camp in the summer. Adam knew that the money his parent had given him for just this one day of skiing, to pay for the chair lift and the rental of the skis, was equal to a day of his father's salary. 'Skiing had better not become a habit,' warned his mother when he left this morning. 'It's too expensive.'

Adam shoved off. He tried to remember Tracey's advice of turning on top of the mogul while at the same time keeping his skis from going out of control. Finally he decided just to get down the hill in his own snowplough style.

At the bottom of the hill, he could see Tracey and Jesse waiting for him.

CHAPTER 4

DUNGEONS AND DRAGONS IN A MALL

They drove back to the city. 'Do you kids mind if I give you money to go have hamburgers in the mall?' Jesse's mom asked. 'You can hang out there for a couple of hours, okay?'

'Mom, we were going to play Dungeons and Dragons,' said Jesse.

'Can't you play it another time?' asked Jesse's mother.

'Sure,' said Tracey quickly.

Jesse shot her a dirty look. 'Don't you care about our Dungeons and Dragons game?' he asked.

'I do,' said Tracey. 'But I'm tired from skiing, anyhow. I don't mind hanging around the mall. I don't get to do it too often.'

'Adam does. He lives so close to the mall, he can walk,' said Jesse.

Adam cringed. Something in Jesse's tone made him feel as if it weren't quite right to live so close to the mall. In fact, Adam realised that most of the more wealthy houses were in more secluded neighbourhoods.

'Adam, what do you want to do?' Jesse asked.

'I don't care,' muttered Adam. 'We can hang around the mall if it's easier.'

'It would make it easier on me,' said Jesse's mom quickly. 'I'll pick you up around nine. You can play some games.'

'I'd rather play Dungeons and Dragons.'

'We can make up a Dungeons and Dragons scenario in a mall,' said Tracey. 'This will be research.'

Adam laughed. He could just imagine a treasure hunt using a mall for a maze.

'That's a great idea. Nobody ever said Dungeons and Dragons always had to be played in the Middle Ages. We can do a modern version.'

Jesse's mother laughed. 'You kids have great imaginations.' She stopped at the Hillside Shopping Mall. 'I'll pick you up at the Sheridan Street entrance.' She reached into her pocketbook and pulled out twenty dollars. 'Here, Jesse, share this with your friends. You can play as many games as you want. But be fair.'

Jesse pocketed the money. 'Okay, Mom,' he said, managing to make it sound like a complaint. 'Remember, Adam is spending the night.'

'Of course, I remember. I talked to his folks this morning. Tracey, is it all right with your folks if you don't get home till around ten?'

'It's fine, Margaret. I'll call them from in here and let them know where I am. See ya later.'

Jesse's mom smiled at Tracey. She drove off. Jesse's eyes followed the sky-blue Volvo until it disappeared in the parking lot. 'She's meeting someone for a date,' he said.

'So what?' asked Tracey.

'Well, she didn't have to just dump us and sneak off. She could have told me who she was meeting.'

'She didn't sneak off, and maybe she didn't want to tell you who her date was. Anyhow, everyone says that your mom is looking terrific these days, that she's never looked better.'

'Yeah, well, you and Adam can't talk. Neither of you have parents who are divorced.'

'Let's go play some games,' said Adam. 'It's freezing out

here.' They stepped on the rubber mat that caused the huge sliding doors of the mall to open automatically. The Hillsdale Mall was the size of two football fields. At one end there was a musical fountain, and at the other an indoor ice rink. Jesse headed straight for the video games arcade.

He was an ace at almost all video games. First it had been Space Invaders, then Galaxian and Pac-Man. Now his favourite game was Rogue Attack. Jesse wasn't a particularly good athlete, but his reflexes were as quick as a snake's.

Because it was Saturday night, the arcade was full, and the only game free was Space Invaders. Jesse went to get change. 'I hate this game,' said Tracey. 'It's got boring.'

'Come on, Tracey. It's the only choice we've got,' said Adam.

Tracey looked around the arcade nervously. The noise of the blips and beeps was so loud that Adam couldn't hear what she said.

Jesse came back, quarters bulging out of the pocket of his jeans. 'I'll go first because they're my quarters.'

'Fine,' said Adam.

He watched as Jesse settled into a steady rhythm, keeping his position behind the blockade as he shot down invader after invader. Adam enjoyed watching Jesse. It was like watching a master. When the game was finally finished, Jesse was only four hundred points below the highest score.

'Your turn,' said Jesse to Adam. Adam took it, with the familiar sinking feeling he had whenever he played the video games. He couldn't figure out why he was so lousy at them. He was good at sports, and a better than average soccer player. He was fine at baseball. He knew he had good hand-eye coordination, but something about the speed with which the attackers moved in video games unnerved him. He never got high scores. He lost the game within minutes.

Tracey took over. She grabbed the controls firmly, but

25

she really wasn't much better than Adam. Her score was only twenty points above his. Adam was secretly pleased.

Jesse didn't bother to keep his pleasure a secret. 'My turn again,' he said as he fed the machine another quarter.

'Let's wander around the mall a little,' said Tracey. 'Maybe we'll get some ideas for a Dungeons and Dragons scenario.'

'I don't want to leave right now,' said Jesse.

'Well, then Adam and I will wander. We'll meet you back here in a half hour and then let's go eat.'

'I'd rather play,' said Jesse, not looking up from the screen.

'Fine, we'll meet you back here,' said Tracey in a tone of voice that no one could argue with. She grabbed Adam's hand. The artificial lighting in the centre of the mall felt like sunlight compared to the dark of the video game arcade.

'Jesse's going to be mad at us for leaving him alone,' warned Adam.

'He's always mad at something anyhow,' said Tracey. 'I get bored watching him play.'

'I like to watch him, 'cause he's so good. You give him a hard time.'

Tracey shook her long hair as if she couldn't be bothered. Adam followed her. He couldn't help but be grateful for Tracey's friendship. She paved the way for everyone to accept him in Buffalo. The first day he arrived at St Luke's she found out he played chess. She challenged him. He beat her but not easily. She announced they were going to be friends. She said she was waiting for someone from California to come and be her friend and be able to beat her at chess. Adam didn't know if she was teasing him or not. Sometimes he still couldn't tell whether Tracey was teasing or not, but he was never bored around her. It felt weird to have a girl as a best friend. He and Tracey weren't going together. They were just best friends; at least that's what Tracey told him they were.

In San Francisco Adam had played with lots of kids

rather than having one best friend. Tracey took some getting used to. She seemed willing to talk to Adam about whatever was on her mind. She'd tell him things about her parents, or about who she didn't like and why. Sometimes Adam didn't know what to say to her. It was as if Tracey never had a thought that she didn't feel free to say out loud.

Everyone talked about Tracey's brilliance. Some people said that she was the most brilliant student to go through St Luke's in a century. But Adam had heard people call him brilliant, too, and brilliance didn't impress him. Everyone called Adam a genius, too. But 'everyone' wasn't his best friend. Tracey was. Nobody else in their class was best friends with someone of the opposite sex. When Adam finally got the courage to ask Tracey how they could be best friends and not go together, she said, 'So what?'

'"So what" isn't an answer,' said Adam.

'Do you want to go together?' Tracey asked suspiciously.

'No,' said Adam honestly. He much preferred having Tracey as a friend.

'Then "so what!" to all those stupid people who think a boy and girl can't just be friends.'

Sometimes Adam called her So What Griffith. It was her favourite expression. She could get away with doing and saying things to other people that nobody else could. If it were anyone except Tracey, they'd slap that kid down for being rude. Tracey could say 'so what' and no one ever answered her.

They wandered from one end of the mall to the other.

'Where do you want to go?' asked Tracey.

'We could go back and watch Jesse,' Adam suggested.

'Naw, he'll still be racking up his high scores. The arcade gives me a headache.'

'It's just because it's the one thing that you're not good at. You shouldn't pick on Jesse. He's great at those games.'

'I don't pick on him.'

'You do too, you know. It's not his fault that his parents are divorced.'

'I don't blame him for *that*. Plenty of kids have divorced

parents. I like Margaret.'

Adam didn't feel comfortable calling Jesse's mother Margaret. Instead he got by with saying thank you and please – quickly.

'Let's go in there,' said Adam, pointing to the electronics store. Adam loved computer stores, particularly this one. Because the Hillsdale Mall was within walking distance of his home, sometimes he would wheel Alison over in her stroller and just look at personal computers.

Tracey followed him inside. The store was divided into sections: stereos, electronic games, small appliances, telephone answering machines, and computers. But each section was small. The entire store was no more than twenty-two by eighteen feet, and only one salesperson was available. Adam wished he could buy everything in the store.

'Can I help you?' asked the saleswoman.

'We're just looking,' said Tracey, flashing the woman a smile. 'My father is thinking of buying my brother and me a computer, and he wanted us to check some of them. Could you show us one?'

Adam blushed. Tracey already had a home computer, and they certainly weren't brother and sister, but Tracey lied so naturally that the saleswoman had no trouble believing her.

'I'll be glad to show one to you. This is our basic –' The woman stopped mid-sentence. Tracey had moved over to the display of electronic games.

'Oh hoo, Adam!' exclaimed Tracey in a gushy voice she almost never used. 'Here's one of those chess sets that you said you were interested in.'

'What chess set?' asked Adam.

'He's a chess whiz-kid,' explained Tracey to the saleswoman.

Adam walked over to the display table. Tracey was fingering a tiny six-inch square electronic chess game. It was so tiny it was hard to believe it had a computer inside of it.

'These sets are very popular,' said the saleslady. 'This is our most expensive and advanced model. It costs nearly $400.'

'Try it, Adam,' said Tracey. 'Make a move.'

Adam picked up a pawn and made a basic opening move, moving the pawn forward two spaces.

A voice within the machine spoke up: 'King pawn to bishop three.'

Tracey giggled. 'It's telling you where to move its piece.'

'I know,' said Adam, but he stared at the machine with wonder. The machine made the perfect response to his opening move. It was so hard to believe that there wasn't a tiny person inside the machine.

'Some of them don't talk,' said the saleswoman.

'Mine doesn't,' said Tracey. 'Mine just flashes its moves. I like the talking one much better.'

Adam put down the pawn. 'Thank you very much,' he said. 'But I don't think my *sister* is interested. She's a lousy chess player.' Adam tried hard to keep from laughing as Tracey made a face at him.

'Very few girls are good,' said the saleslady. 'I am.'

Adam looked at her with new interest. 'Can you beat the machine?'

The woman nodded. She was a very pretty woman – a little younger than his mother, with blonde hair. She didn't look at all like a chess player. She seemed shy.

'We have to go now,' said Tracey in her most affected private school accent. 'We'll come in with my father later. Come along, Sebastian.'

Before they left, Adam turned to the saleswoman. 'Thank you for your help,' he said.

'Good luck with your chess game,' she said.

Outside of the store, Adam went and sat at the edge of the fountain in the middle of the mall. 'What did you do that for?' he asked.

'What?' asked Tracey innocently.

'Make up that story about us being brother and sister, and telling her my name was Sebastian.'

Tracey shrugged. 'Maybe you should be Sebastian.'

Adam shook his head. 'You're crazy, you know.'

'Come on, what harm did it do, and if I hadn't made up that story, she might have kicked us out. It was a goof.'

'Well, it made me feel creepy to lie.'

'Oh, Adam, you're such a goody-goody.'

CHAPTER 5

GORGONZOLA'S REVENGE

Adam woke up to a voice in his ear saying, 'Adam Rosenbaum, you are wanted for murder. You have the right to remain silent while your toenails are pulled from your toes, one by one.'

Adam sat upright in bed, not quite sure whether he was dreaming or not. Shadows played on the wall. He was alone in the guest room in Jesse's house. Jesse couldn't stand to have anyone else sleep in his room. When friends slept over at Adam's house, they stayed in his room with him. But Jesse was different. Some of their friends thought it was weird to have to sleep in the guest room, but Adam didn't mind. In truth, he liked sleeping on the huge pull-out sofa bed. The guest room even had its own TV.

Adam looked at the clock radio next to the sofa bed. 5:46 AM The room was silent. He decided that he must have dreamed the strange voice.

Then he heard a whirring noise. 'You have willfully committed murder, and now you will die painfully.' The voice seemed to be coming from the clock radio.

'Gorgonzola the Magnificent must have his revenge,' said the radio.

Now Adam knew that Jesse had somehow rigged the

machine. Gorgonzola the Magnificent was Jesse's character in their Dungeons and Dragons game, a dwarf with
great infravision but a chaotic creature whom Adam's
character had killed in their last scenario.

Adam lifted the radio. It was thin and tiny, fitting easily
into his hand, but he noticed that it had a cassette recorder
built into it. Adam had never seen anything like it. He lay
back on his pillow and waited. The tape continued.

'After the ghost of Gorgonzola has finished with your
toenails, he will proceed to pull out your fingernails, and
then your curly hair. You will be forced to lie naked on top
of an anthill, and Gorgonzola will spread his special
cheese all over you to encourage the ants to eat you. Good
morning.'

Adam heard the click as the tape shut itself off. He
picked up the clock radio again and pushed the eject
button. The tape came out in his hand. The machine
could be set to play a tape at any time. Adam supposed it
had been designed for people who wanted to wake up to
thier own choice of music. Adam held the tape in his hand,
wondering if Jesse was awake and waiting for his reaction.

He opened the door of the guest room. The door to
Jesse's room was ajar. Adam pushed it farther open. Jesse's
jeans lay on the floor. His hockey stick rested on his tape
deck. Posters of John Lennon covered the wall. Jesse was a
Lennon freak, and he knew more details of Lennon's
murder than anyone else. He always wrote themes on John
Lennon whenever he got the chance. Lennon's gentle but
slightly maniacal smile leered down at Adam, along with
a blowup of Lennon's broken glasses that Yoko had
photographed after the murder.

Jesse was sound asleep. Adam looked down at his friend.
Jesse looked sweaty and damp, even though the room was
cool. His tongue hung slightly outside of his mouth.
Adam felt strange watching a friend sleep. Awake, Jesse
moved jerkily, except when standing in front of a video
game; but asleep he looked soft. Adam tiptoed over to
Jesse's tape deck and studied it. A tape was in, and an open

tape case lay on top of the deck. Adam rummaged around and found a crumpled-up piece of paper with 'Gorgon-zola's Revenge' written on it. Adam had to admit it had been a pretty good joke.

He glanced back at Jesse, who turned in his sleep, taking his pillow with him, hugging it to his chest. He looked like Alison with her stuffed unicorn.

Adam started to tiptoe out of Jesse's room. He no longer felt like waking him up. Then he halted. Jesse's hand dangled over his bed; Adam decided that he had to do *something* to pay Jesse back for rigging up the clock radio to scare him.

Adam looked at Jesse's hand. He remembered his father telling him that if you put a guy's hand in warm water while he was sleeping it would make him pee.

Adam smiled to himself. Jesse's room had its own bathroom. Adam tiptoed into it and closed the door. He looked around for something to hold the water. A glass would be too small to fit Jesse's hand. Adam needed something larger. He spotted the wastepaper basket made up of strips of mirror pasted against a tin base. The mirrror reflected weird angles of light as Adam picked it up. He filled it up with warm water, not too hot. He tested the water with his elbow, the way he tested Alison's bath. The water felt right. He worried that the sound of running water would wake Jesse.

The basket was so heavy with the water inside it that Adam could barely lift it. He opened the bathroom door slowly. Jesse's hand still hung over the side of the bed.

Adam carried the basket to the bed, sloshing a tiny bit of water on the floor. Very carefully he lifted Jesse's hand and dipped it in the water. Jesse groaned in his sleep.

Adam waited, crouched by the side of Jesse's bed. Several seconds passed, and each second felt like five minutes. Adam realised he was holding his breath.

Then suddenly Jesse was sitting up in bed, flinging off the covers, dashing for the bathroom. He tripped on the wastebasket, sending water across the floor. Jesse swore and crashed toward the bathroom, the front and legs of his pj's wet.

Adam immediately felt guilty. The look on Jesse's face was one of shock and almost horror. Adam wished that he hadn't been tempted by Jesse's dangling hand. He tried to pick Jesse's clothes up off the floor so they wouldn't get soaked.

'Hey, Jesse, throw me a towel,' Adam whispered into the bathroom. Jesse refused to answer. 'Come on, Jesse,' whispered Adam urgently, 'everything's getting wet.'

Jesse came out of the bathroom with a towel wrapped around his waist. He stalked angrily to his dresser drawer and pulled out the bottoms to another pair of pj's.

'Jess, it was just a joke,' whispered Adam. He had expected Jesse to get mad and then laugh. Jesse slammed the dresser drawer shut.

Adam went into the bathroom and got a towel. He tried to wipe up the water, but it seemed to be seeping into every corner of the room. Jesse sat on the edge of his bed, not lifting a finger to help. Adam crawled around on his hands and knees, whipping the towel along the floor. The towel was soon soaked through, and Adam carried it into the bathroom and flung it into a corner of the bathtub.

He came back out into Jesse's bedroom. Jesse hadn't moved. 'Hey, Jesse,' said Adam, aware that he had a stupid, nervous mile on his face. 'How d'you like my revenge for Gorgonzola's revenge?'

CHAPTER 6

BLACKMAIL

Jesse continued to stare into space, refusing to meet Adam's eyes. 'Why did you do that to me?' Jesse asked in a flat voice.

'Hey, come on!' objected Adam. He already felt guilty enough. 'You were the one who made the Gorgonzola tape that woke me up in the middle of the night.'

Jesse wiped a hand across his face and still said nothing. Adam stared up at him. He thought, but wasn't sure, that Jesse was crying.

'Jesse?' he asked tentatively. Jesse sniffed and turned his face halfway to the wall. Adam cleaned up the rest of the spilled water and brought the wastepaper basket back into the bathroom. He saw Jesse's pyjama bottoms soaking in the sink.

Adam felt terrible. It wasn't even six in the morning, and he had visions of Jesse sulking all day.

Adam went back out into Jesse's bedroom and decided to try to explain again. 'Jesse, it was just an old joke my father told me about. I never had a chance to try it out. Your hand was just dangling there. Besides, you were the creep that rigged that radio to wake me up, so why are you so mad?'

'What are you talking about?' Jesse asked, turning to face Adam for the first time.

'Gorgonzola the Magnificent! The revenge! Come on, don't play dumb. I was asleep, and all of a sudden there was this creepy voice in my ear.'

Jesse smiled. 'It worked, didn't it? I once made a tape that woke my mom up and she almost killed me.'

'What did it say?' Adam asked.

'Never mind.' Jesse laughed. 'So I really got you with that tape? What did you think was happening?'

Adam knew what Jesse wanted to hear. 'I thought I was having a bad dream,' he said. 'A real nightmare. Then finally I figured out where the voice was coming from.'

'Yeah, I should have hid the clock radio. That would have been even better.'

'Anyhow,' said Adam, 'you can't blame me for wanting to get even.'

Jesse's eyes turned into slits. 'How did you get even?' he asked. Something about his tone of voice scared Adam.

'Look, I already said I was sorry about sticking your hand in the water, but it was pretty funny. My dad told me that if you stick someone's hand in a bucket of warm water it will make them pee. Wait until he hears that it worked.'

'I'll kill you if you tell your dad,' said Jesse, sounding serious.

'Hey, Jesse, I said I was sorry about a million times.'

'Are you trying to tell me that I peed because you stuck my hand in a bucket?'

'It wasn't actually a bucket. It was really your wastepaper basket. But sure, that's what happened. Where did you think all that water came from?'

'Sometimes I wet my bed,' whispered Jesse. 'I thought you knew, and you were just waiting to see if I would do it. I thought I wet my bed by myself, and you happened to catch me.'

Adam swallowed hard. He felt ugly and wished with all his heart that he were someplace else. 'I wouldn't have played that stupid joke on you if I knew ...' Adam's voice

36

trailed off. 'Honest, Jess, you've got to believe me. I wouldn't be that mean.'

Jesse looked miserable, and Adam felt as bad as Jesse looked. The sun was just rising, and Adam could see streaks of orange in the sky. 'Look, Jesse, the sun's coming up. Forget about it. I promise I won't tell anyone.'

Jesse hardly gave the sunrise a second look. 'Tell me something about yourself that you don't want anybody to know,' he said. 'Then I'll be sure you won't tell.'

Adam thought for a moment. He flashed on Tracey saying, 'Oh, Adam, you're such a goody-goody.' He couldn't think of what to tell Jesse.

'Well!' Jesse demanded.

'Look, you don't need to blackmail me. Trust me. I really won't tell anyone.'

'It's not blackmail. But if I'm supposed to trust you with my secret, you have to tell me a secret.'

Adam sighed. He *felt* blackmailed, and he didn't know what to say. He couldn't think of anything that would satisfy Jesse. In fact, the most embarrassing thing that he could think of was that he didn't have dirty secrets. But he didn't think Jesse would accept that.

'Okay,' he said slowly. 'When I was in San Francisco I hung out with a bunch of kids who stole a lot.'

'Did you steal?' Jesse asked.

'Yes,' answered Adam.

'What did you steal?' Jesse asked. 'If you tell me you filched some dinky candy bars, I'll kill you.'

'No, this was an organised gang. We actually stole an Atari computer.'

'You're kidding!' said Jesse, sounding very excited. 'How could you do that'

'At night,' Adam said. 'We hid in the store until closing. You kow how computer stores are used to kids hanging out.'

'But stealing something worth that much is a real felony,' said Jesse.

'I know,' said Adam. 'That's why I've never told anyone

that we did it. You're the only one in all of Buffalo who knows.'

Jesse seemed satisfied. Adam felt creepy. The story was a lie. He had never stolen anything in his life.

Adam looked out the window again. The early morning light gave a soft glow to the snow. 'It's just getting light out,' he said. 'We could go play in the snow. It'll be neat at dawn.'

Jesse pulled up the covers. 'I don't want to play in the snow. Besides, we have to be quiet. My mom will kill us if we wake her up now. Why don't you go back to sleep.'

Adam felt wide-awake, and he resented Jesse's attitude. Jesse seemed to have forgotten that he was the one that had started it all by setting the clock radio for 5:46 AM.

'What time do you normally have breakfast around here?' Adam asked.

'Around nine on Sunday,' said Jesse, turning his back to Adam.

Adam returned to the guest room. He knew he would never get back to sleep. He lay on the bed and reread one of Jesse's Dungeons and Dragons Quest books.

Finally, he heard the sounds of Jesse's mother getting up, and a little while later, Jesse knocked on his door. 'Come on,' said Jesse. 'Let's get some breakfast.'

After breakfast, Adam continued to feel creepy and awkward. He didn't know what to do with himself, and Jesse wasn't much help. 'Do you want to play chess?' Adam asked Jesse. Jesse's head was buried in the comics.

'Naw, not now,' said Jesse.

'Well, what do you want to do?' asked Adam.

'Nothing,' said Jesse.

Jesse's mother looked up from doing the crossword puzzle. 'Jesse, Adam's your guest.'

'Well, I don't feel like playing. We already took him skiing and fooling around in the mall.'

'Jesse!' said his mother sharply. 'That's very rude.'

'It's okay,' said Adam. 'Jesse got up on the wrong side of the bed. I'm okay.'

'You're more than okay, Adam,' said Jesse's mother. 'You're a very understanding kid. Jesse could learn a lot from you. Why don't you play with one of Jesse's games? You're a chess freak, aren't you? Why don't you try the Chess Challenger? Jesse has one of those chess computers you can play with by yourself.'

'Do you have one of those chess computers like Tracey's?' asked Adam.

Jesse lifted his head out of the comics. 'I'll get it for you. I'm sorry I was rude before.' Adam couldn't tell whether or not Jesse was saying that for the benefit of his mother.

Jesse brought down his chess machine. It was amazingly small for such a complicated game. Adam played a game against the machine. The machine made some unexpected moves that kept him on his toes, but in the end Adam beat the machine. 'This machine is terrific,' said Adam.

'There's an even better one that they put out now,' said Jesse. 'It talks and tells you what move it wants to make.'

'I know,' said Adam. 'Tracey and I saw it in the mall when you were playing the games yesterday.'

'I asked my mom to get me that one for my birthday,' said Jesse. 'If she gets me it, I'll let you have this one.'

Adam looked down at the machine. He wanted a chess computer, but he didn't want a hand-me-down. He wanted the one that talked, too. It didn't seem fair that Tracey and Jesse could have anything they wanted and he couldn't. He was the best player of the three of them. He was the one who had the right to the best chess computer. But since he'd already asked his parents for one, he knew they couldn't afford it. It seemed that everything Adam wanted, they could not afford.

CHAPTER 7

A STUPID LIE

At noon, Adam's father came to pick him up. Adam was ready to leave. He still felt awkward with Jesse. But Adam's father seemed in no hurry. He stood in the foyer of Jesse's house in his jeans and brown down jacket, apologising for dripping snow.

'I'll be right there, Dad,' said Adam. 'You don't have to take your boots off.'

Adam's father gave him a puzzled look. Usually he had to pry Adam away from Jesse's house. 'How was the skiing yesterday?' Adam's dad asked.

'Great,' said Adam, picking up his backpack.

Jesse's mom stood on the staircase, looking down. 'Richard, come on, have a cup of coffee and warm up.'

'I'd love one,' said Adam's father.

'Dad, I've got to get home and do my homework,' said Adam.

'Just one cup. It's cold out there. I forgot about Buffalo winters.'

Adam watched his father take off his jacket and hang it up. Jesse's mother came out of the kitchen holding two mugs of coffee. 'Did you know that your dad and I grew up together? We used to date.'

Adam glanced up at his father, who seemed to be blushing under his beard. 'Of course, that was before he became a hippie,' added Jesse's mother with a laugh.

'Only in Buffalo would becoming a grade-school teacher be called being a hippie,' said Adam's father.

'Well, everyone did expect you to become a doctor like your father.'

'That's why I left home.'

Adam glanced at Jesse, who was listening intently. Adam wished they would leave. 'How come you came back to Buffalo?' Jesse asked. 'California sounds so neat.'

'It was, but I couldn't get a good job there. When I found out that St Luke's had a job for both me and my wife, we decided to give it a try.'

'Come on, now,' said Jesse's mother in a teasing voice. 'Homecoming hasn't been all that bad.' She turned to Adam. 'You seem to be adjusting to Buffalo pretty well, particularly the way you ski. Do you miss California?'

'Some,' said Adam. 'But I like it here, too.'

Jesse's mother looked up at Adam's father as if she had won a point in a tennis match. 'See, your son likes it here.'

Adam's father winked at Adam. 'I like it, too, Margaret. We're not unhappy here.' He seemed to emphasise the 'we'. He took a long sip of the coffee. 'Come on, Adam, let's get going.'

'Your wife doesn't ski, does she?' asked Jesse's mother.

'No,' said Adam's father.

'But you used to be a great skier,' said Jesse's mother. 'Maybe one of these weekends, you'll come with Adam and Jesse and me.'

Adam stared at his father. He distinctly remembered his father telling him that he never skied. 'Adam, get your things together,' he said quickly. 'Thank Margaret for taking you skiing and having you for the night.'

Margaret laughed. 'Adam's already thanked me a couple of times for the skiing and dinner last night. You've raised one of the most polite kids I've ever met.'

'Not me. Grace and I together. Come on, Adam.'

Adam picked up his knapsack and said good-bye to Jesse. 'I'll talk to you later,' he said.

Adam's father laughed. 'The two of you just spent nearly thirty hours together, and you're going to see each other in class in the morning. Still, you're going to talk!'

'You remember, that's the age that you start growing a telephone in your ear,' said Jesse's mom. 'Remember, you and I used to spend hours on the phone.'

'But that was in high school,' protested Adam's father.

'It started in seventh grade,' said Jesse's mother.

Outside, Adam flung his knapsack into the back-seat of the car. It landed on Alison's empty baby seat. Adam looked straight out the window, feeling nervous.

His father drove, concentrating on the road. 'Come on, Adam, out with it. You want to know why I lied to you and told you I couldn't ski, don't you?'

Adam turned to face his father. 'It was a stupid lie.'

'I know. That's why I want to talk to you about it.'

'Does Mom know you used to date Jesse's mom?' Adam asked.

'That sounds like a trick question on Family Feud.'

'It's not a joke.'

'I know. Adam, I'm sorry. Yes, Mom knows who I used to date, and she knows I used to go out with Jesse's mom. When I met your mom, I used to entertain her with stories about growing up in Buffalo. It was very different from growing up in California.'

'And what about the lie you told me? You told me that you couldn't ski.'

'That one I feel bad about. It's just that when I moved to California, I decided I hated skiing. It costs so much money. Only rich people can do it.'

'That's not true,' protested Adam.

'Okay, rich and middle class people can do it. But you don't see many poor people skiing.'

'That doesn't make it bad, does it?' asked Adam.

'No, what's bad is lying to your kid for stupid reasons. I just never told your mom that I knew how to ski. When we

42

came back here, I should have realised that you'd want to ski, that all your friends would ski, It would have been easier to have just told you the truth, but I had already told the silly lie to Mom and you, so I just kept it up. I guess I felt ambivalent. It means that you feel two things at once about something. I wanted to come back to Buffalo, but I was a little afraid of being back in the place where I once was a kid.'

Adam picked up an old Rubik's Cube he had left lying on the dashboard. His father always seemed to find it easier to talk to him in the car. Maybe because he had to keep his eye on the road, and he didn't have to look Adam in the face. Adam didn't understand all that his father had said. He couldn't understand why his father had told such a stupid lie. Why tell him that he didn't ski when he was good at it? Then Adam remembered his lie to Jesse. Why had he told Jesse that he had stolen a computer?

Adam turned his Cube round and round, the clicks the only sounds in the car. He could do the Cube in less than five minutes, and the feel of it in his hand satisfied him.

'Adam, tell me what you're thinking. Don't keep it bottled up inside.'

'I'm not thinking. I'm playing with my Cube.'

'I'm sorry I lied to you about the skiing. I honestly can't explain it very well.'

Adam shrugged. After all, he was lying about not thinking. He was thinking hard; he just didn't know what to say to his father. Why? Adam wanted to know why. Why did they have less money than most of the other kids at St Luke's? Why didn't his father *want* to ski? Skiing was wonderful, even if it was expensive. But Adam felt that his father would be hurt if he asked him those questions.

'What did you guys do after skiing?' asked Adam's father. 'Did you play Dungeons and Dragons?'

'No. Jesse's mom had a date.' Adam felt good about telling his father that. 'She let us out at the mall and we hung around there. Jesse played some video games. Tracey and I just hung out.'

'Didn't you eat?'

'Sure, Jesse's mom gave us money to buy hamburgers.'

'We gave you money,' said Adam's father sharply. 'You shouldn't have let Jesse pay.'

'I didn't have much money left after I paid for my skis and for the lift ticket, and I had to buy lunch. Besides, if we had eaten at Jesse's house, his mom would have paid. She said dinner was her treat. Tracey didn't say anything when Jesse paid.'

'I don't care what Tracey Griffith does. You pay your own way.'

Adam clenched his teeth, but he didn't say anything. The *click click* of his Cube was once again the only sound in the car.

They arrived home, and Adam's mouth literally fell open. His mother was out on the front lawn, rolling a huge ball of snow toward the centre of the lawn.

She waved. Alison was outside in her snowsuit, bending over and eating snow.

'What's Mom doing?' Adam asked.

'What does it look like?' asked Adam's father.

'Building a snowman?' said Adam incredulously, because it seemed like something that he would never imagine his mother doing. Her long black hair was caked with snow. She ran to the car and opened the door. 'It was so beautiful out, I couldn't stay inside a minute longer. Come on, I need your help.'

Adam put his Cube on the dashboard and got out of the car. '*You* are building a snowman, Mom?'

Adam's mother laughed. 'Well, a snowperson, or maybe she's a snowlady. It's too early to tell. Anyhow, Alison woke up from her nap while your dad was picking you up. I could tell nothing would keep her from the snow. Then I realised I had never built a snowman ... snowperson – in my life.'

'But, Mom, this isn't like you,' said Adam.

Adam's mother picked up some snow, packed it into a snowball, and rifled it right at Adam's chest. 'Listen,

44

sonny, those are fighting words.'

Adam studied her face to see if she was serious. She seemed to be laughing. But quite honestly, Adam felt confused. His mother usually said that she hated the outdoors. Even in California when all her friends were into running, aerobic dance exercise, and hiking, Adam's mother said that whenever she felt the need to exercise, she walked to a bookshelf. Seeing her out in the snow seemed so out of character.

'Come on, Adam,' said Adam's father. 'We might as well get into the act.'

The three of them made an enormous snowperson, over seven feet high. Alison kept shrieking every time they rolled one of the huge balls of snow near her. Soon the lawn looked as if an enormous tank had been through, making large, wide tracks.

Adam was too short to help in the raising of the head. His mother and father balanced the head between them. They almost dropped it, but they finally got it on the body in a half lopsided position.

'Yea!' shouted Adam, stepping back to admire it. His parents kissed in front of the snowman. Then in the middle of their embrace, Adam's father stuck out his foot and tumbled Adam's mother into the snow. She laughed and grabbed some snow and rubbed it into Adam's father's beard. Alison fell on top of them. Adam stood to the side, not sure what to do, feeling slightly embarrassed.

Adam's father caught him by the ankle and dragged him down on top. 'Let me go!' yelled Adam, but he was laughing. He couldn't tell whether it was his mother's or father's arms that encircled him. Alison was somewhere in the middle like a sandwich. They rolled over in the snow, and Adam found himself laughing so hard that he couldn't stop.

CHAPTER 8

AN ELEGANT AND EXCELLENT PLAN

Adam had trouble sleeping that night. Usually he had a surefire way of going to sleep: He played a chess game in his head. But tonight he couldn't fall asleep. He thought about the long day, the trick he had played on Jesse, his father's lie, the making of the snowman.

For almost the first time since they had moved, Adam wished he were back in California. At least in California, Adam rarely thought about money. Most of his friends back there didn't have much more than he did. But in Buffalo, it was different. It was different going to a private school.

Adam willed himself to stop thinking. He tried to set up the imaginary chessboard in his head. However, instead of the usual large chessboard that he liked to imagine, he kept seeing the tiny brown-and-white squares of Jesse's chess computer.

Adam was sick of everyone telling him that life was unfair. 'Enough already,' he thought to himself. It wasn't fair that he had to learn that lesson so many times when someone like Tracey didn't have to learn it at all. It wasn't fair that he couldn't make money from other baby-sitting jobs. It wasn't fair that Tracey, Jesse, and most of the other kids at St Luke's had so much money that they never had to think about it.

Adam rolled over, twisting his blanket around him. He wanted that chess computer, not the crummy hand-me-down from Jesse. He wanted the ultimate Chess Challenger, the one that he and Tracey had seen in the store. It was tiny. It could easily fit into a knapsack.

Adam thought about the lie he had told Jesse. Would he really have the nerve to steal anything? Jesse had looked at him with such respect when Adam lied about stealing the computer.

Suppose he were the kind of kid who would steal something like that. How would he do it? When Adam played chess, he was famous for his crafty moves. He would never attack an oppenent's chess piece directly. He would use his pawns like decoys to test for traps.

Adam lay on his back and stared at his ceiling. Just suppose he were going to steal the chess computer from the computer store. Adam felt as if he were splitting in two. One part of his mind warned, 'Don't even think about it.' The other part said, 'Go ahead. You're just a kid lying in bed at night. There's no law against thinking about stealing. There's no law against thinking up a plan.'

Adam told himself it was all right to map out a plan for stealing the computer because he would never do it.

'All right, now,' thought Adam to himself. 'I can't steal it myself because the saleslady might recognise me. She's seen me lots of times. Even if I wore a ski mask, she'd know I was a kid. She might remember that Tracey and I were in there asking about the Chess Challenger. One of the rules of chess is to use a disadvantage into a point of power. I've got to find some way of using the fact that she knows me to my advantage. Make her think that I'm the last person in the world who would steal something from her.'

Adam thought hard. He loved to think up strategies. He was an excellent Dungeons and Dragons player. In Dungeons and Dragons, a character had to find the treasure without endangering his or her own life. Adam decided that the chess computer was like the treasure in a Dungeons and Dragons game. In Dungeons and Dragons, as in chess, the smartest move was often the exact opposite of the most obvious move.

'If I were a real thief, what is the opposite move?' Adam asked himself. He grinned to himself as the answer came to him. 'I would return something to the store. I could take something and then return it, telling the saleslady that it had fallen into my bag by mistake. Then I'd be in the clear. I would be remembered as the boy who did not steal.'

Adam felt himself get excited and hot and sweaty in the bed. He could see himself returning something to the saleslady. He could hear praising him. 'What a nice boy,' she would say.

Adam forced his mind to go on to the next problem. What should he steal for the decoy? It had to be something small.

Suddenly Adam's mind made a mental leap, the kind of leap he occasionally made in a chess game, a brilliant leap. A leap like that made him feel invincible. He knew how he would steal the chess computer. It was a foolproof plan, a plan so complicated that nobody he knew would think of it.

He knew exactly what he would steal from the store. The tiny clock radio with the tape deck, just like the one at Jesse's house. His mind raced. He was in love with his plan.

First he would steal the tape/clock radio. He would only need to have it in his possession for a short while. He would go to the far end of the mall and tape a message on the machine, a threatening message.

BEWARE, YOU WILL BE HURT
IF YOU DO NOT DO AS I SAY.
GO TO THE BATHROOM AND
LOCK THE DOOR.

Then he would set the machine for any time he pleased,

48

just like an alarm clock. He could return the machine to the store and leave free as a bird. All he would have to do was to go back at the correct time and the saleslady would be locked in the bathroom. He could sneak in and take the Chess Challenger and be out of there before she got the nerve to come out of the bathroom.

'It's a beautiful plan,' thought Adam. Only a real genius could think of something so clever. Adam loved his mind for thinking it up.

He went over the plan to see if there were any flaws. Wait a minute. Suppose the saleslady recognised his voice on the tape? And he wasn't sure that the clock radio could actually record tapes. It played tapes, but it might not record them. In fact, it was obvious that Jesse had recorded his message on his tape deck. Luckily, his father did have a portable tape recorder. He used it in his first grade class to record the stories that his students made up. Adam would be able to talk his father into letting him borrow it.

Now all he would have to do was disguise his voice. Adam thought. His mind didn't fail him. He came up with a beautiful plan. He wouldn't even have to use his own voice. They'd never be able to connect him with the theft. A perfect plan. Adam tried to calm himself down. He felt as if he would never fall asleep.

He reminded himself that it was just a head game. He would never try to execute the plan. But his mind raced on into the night, going over the plan again and again. It felt delicious. Adam knew that the mathematicians sometimes called their work 'elegant'. 'An elegant solution.' Well, Adam thought that his plan was elegant. An elegant and excellent plan, that's what it was.

CHAPTER 9

NOTHING BUT THE BEST

At breakfast the next morning, Adam tried to remind himself that his plan was like a dream, best forgotten in the light of day. But he couldn't forget it. He felt as if fate was conspiring to make it easy for him to put the plan in force.

First his mother turned to him at breakfast and said, 'Adam, I hate to ask you, but Dad and I need you to take care of Alison again. We have to go to a meeting for the disarmament rally we're planning for the spring. If you want, you can bring Tracey and Jesse and some of the kids over to play with you.'

Adam took another bite of his cereal. His father glanced at him and seemed to take his silence for resentment. 'I know it's a drag, Adam. But it's for a good cause. After all, we're trying to make sure there's a world left for you and Alison to grow up into.'

Adam's mother pulled her heavy hair away from her face. She smiled at Adam. 'Dad didn't mean to give you a lecture.'

'No, no,' said Adam quickly. 'It's okay. I don't mind. Only I was thinking. Alison's so cooped up during the winter. Why don't I take care of her at the mall? They have

50

an indoor playground.'

Alison heard her name mentioned. 'Alison want to go to playground!' she shouted.

'Alison, we heard you. You want to go to the mall.' He looked at Adam's mother, but he spoke to Adam. 'Did you really think I was lecturing you?'

'You sounded as if you were talking to a class, not to your son,' said Adam's mother.

'I asked him, not you.'

'I already said that I don't mind,' said Adam quickly. 'I can pick Alison up at the day-care centre, and we can walk to the mall. It's not far.' Adam took a breath. He wanted to sound as casual as possible. 'By the way, Dad, would it be all right if I borrowed your portable tape recorder today? I want to use it for our Dungeons and Dragons game, but I will be terribly careful with it. I won't let anyone else touch it.'

Adam's father shook his head. 'Adam, sometimes you sound like sixty instead of twelve.'

Adam didn't like his father's tone of voice, but he wanted the tape recorder. He picked up his cereal bowl and took it to the sink. 'I've got some things I've got to do to get ready for school. Is it okay for me to borrow the tape recorder?'

Adam's father sighed. 'Of course, I'm sure you'll take better care of it than I would. It's on my desk.'

As Adam left the room, he could hear his mother say, 'You shouldn't tease him all the time.'

'I wasn't teasing. He knows I love him.'

'Yeah, but what a double message. I love you, but you act like an old man.' Adam's mother sounded really upset.

Adam hated it when his parents argued. In California they never seemed to argue, but in Buffalo, they snapped at each other a lot.

One of the reasons why Adam had loved making the snowman was that his parents had seemed so happy together. He hated it when they argued over him. Adam glanced out the window and at the snowman. He was still

51

there. He looked like a drawing out of a children's book.

Adam paused. Had he really convinced his parents to drop him off at the mall? Was he really going to borrow his father's tape recorder? Was he going to steal the machine? Adam, the little old man of a kid who was *so* responsible?

Adam wondered what his father would do if he knew what Adam planned, if he knew that his wonderful little boy was thinking of becoming a very clever thief.

Adam went up to his room. He felt as if he were a robot programmed to continue. He took out a pile of index cards and wrote a single word on each card.

BE

WARE

YOU

WILL

BE

HURT

IF

YOU

DO

NOT

DO

AS

I

SAY

GO

TO

THE

BATHROOM

AND

LOCK

THE

DOOR.

He printed the words very carefully, almost giggling to himself. Twenty-two words. Twenty-two people would help him steal, but none of them would know. Oh, the plan was truly delicious.

He put the cards into the pocket of his knapsack and went into his parents' room and looked for the tape recorder. His father's desk was full of children's drawings from his class. Up on the wall was a large colour photograph of Adam as a baby in Golden Gate Park in San Francisco. Adam stared at the picture. The baby looked so innocent and happy. It was hard to believe he had ever been so little. His thighs were fat and wrinkled, chubby little thighs. His hands were high in the air, and he had an expression of absolute glee on his face.

Adam found the tape recorder and stuffed it into his knapsack. He told himself that a gleeful baby like that deserved the best.

CHAPTER 10

DOOMSDAY SCENARIO

All day in school Adam couldn't concentrate. His teachers didn't notice. Adam was such a good student that he knew his teachers would let him coast for a day, but Tracey noticed.

'Hey, Adam, what's wrong?' she asked.

'Wrong? What do you mean?' Adam felt weird, and he hadn't actually stolen anything yet.

'Weird, weird! Like you're not here.'

'I'm there.'

'Where's there?'

'Here.'

'Well, if you're here, you can't be there.' Tracey laughed and Adam laughed with her, but his laugh sounded wrong even to him.

'You still sound nervous. You have a nervous laugh.'

'I do not,' said Adam, but then he gave a half laugh, and he knew he sounded nervous. Well, Tracey would laugh nervously, too, if she knew what he was planning to do.

'Will you come over this afternoon and play chess?' Tracey asked. 'We haven't had a good game in a while.'

'I can't. I've got to take care of Alison again.'

'That stinks,' said Tracey. 'You have to baby-sit all the

time.'

'Well, Mom and Dad are both working on a disarmament rally.'

'My parents are working on that, too,' said Tracey, suddenly sounding excited. 'Hey, did you know why the pilots who fly the SAC bombers wear eye patches? Those are the pilots that are prepared to go up in the air if they hear that someone has aimed a nuclear bomb at us. They have to fly with an eye patch. It's in their regulations. Guess why.'

'Is this a riddle?'

'No,' said Tracey impatiently. 'It's true. My parents told me about it. The pilots are trained to fly with eye patches. Why?'

Adam thought about it. 'I don't know,' he answered.

'Think!' demanded Tracey. 'I figured it out. You can, too.'

Adam's competitive juices began to flow. His mind felt as if it had been turned on. He pictured the pilot in the huge bomber looking out of the curved plexiglass window of the plane, flying toward Russia, knowing that the world was probably going to end, knowing that millions of people at home were already dead. Adam tried to picture the pilot with a black eye patch. Suddenly Adam got it.

'If there were a nuclear blast while the pilot was up in the air, he or she would be blinded. So if the pilot wore an eye patch and the blast from the enemy's nuclear bombs went off, the pilot would still have one good eye.' Adam felt good about his answer. He knew that nuclear blasts gave off intense light, so intense that at Hiroshima, shadows of dying people and dogs were etched on the ground while nothing of their bodies remained.

'You're right,' said Tracey. 'Isn't that creepy? Mom and Dad want the school to have a study programme on nuclear war. I bet that's what they're working on with your parents.'

'If you thought the end of the world was coming, what would you do?' asked Adam.

Tracey thought. 'Go find Andy Gibb,' she said finally.

'Seriously,' said Adam.

'Well, I'd hate to die a virgin, but I'm too young, so I think I'd just like to die in Andy Gibb's arms. What would you do?'

'I don't know,' said Adam. 'But it makes you think, doesn't it? We may never live to have children.'

'Or even graduate from eighth grade,' added Tracey. 'It's not fair.'

'What's not fair?' asked Jesse and Tiffany. Tiffany was another girl in their class.

'We're talking about what we would do if we knew nuclear war was coming,' said Tracey.

'Die,' said Jesse, and then he laughed nervously.

'I'd try to get home,' said Tiffany, 'and hide out in my cellar.'

'It wouldn't do you any good. Your cellar would disappear in a mist. It would be vapourised. Temperatures get above two thousand degrees.'

'I'd head for the lake,' said Jesse.

'It would be gone,' said Tracey. 'At two thousand degrees everything would boil away. Your flesh would boil right off your bones.'

'Very appetizing.'

'Nuclear war isn't going to be appetizing,' said Tracey.

'Hey, you know what we could do?' said Jesse. 'We could to a whole Dungeons and Dragons scenario based on nuclear war.'

Tracey looked at Jesse with respect. 'You know, that's not a bad project. We could set up a whole maze that would teach kids how bad nuclear war would be. What about it, Adam?'

'Huh?' said Adam, who was feeling more and more out of it.

'What about the kids who don't play Dungeons and Dragons?' asked Pam, who almost never played herself.

'We could make it very simple, the most basic level,' said Jesse. 'We could make a Dungeons and Dragons scenario for everyone. We could make it so that nobody felt left out. It would be like a play, but because it would be based on throwing the dice like in Dungeons and Dragons, it would be more interesting.'

'And more like real life,' said Tracey excitedly. 'Because the people who make the bombs are really throwing a dice with our lives.'

'We could present it at an assembly,' said Tiffany. 'We could get everyone involved.'

'That's a great idea, Tiffany,' said Tracey. 'We could get all the younger kids and older kids involved. The older kids wouldn't think it was silly because it would be like Dungeons and Dragons, and everyone would learn something from it.'

Adam listened to them, but he felt as if he were wrapped in a blanket. He felt he understood why some people were called 'wet blankets'. That's how he felt. Usually he was the one to come up with the best ideas for a Dungeons and Dragons strategy or for a new project. But his mind seemed unable to function. Ever since Tracey started to talk about nuclear war, Adam kept thinking about all the things that he wanted to own before he died.

'Let's start working on it this afternoon,' said Tracey. 'We can go to my house. Adam, you can bring Alison. We'll all help you baby-sit. After all, we want her to be able to live, too. It's not fair for her to be killed in a nuclear war. She's just a baby.'

Adam felt a wave of relief wash over him. If he could make himself get involved in the nuclear disarmament scenario, he wouldn't go to the mall. He wouldn't steal.

'Fine,' said Adam.

'Hey, wait!' said Tiffany. 'I have a dance lesson this afternoon. Can't we do it tomorrow?'

'Yeah, and I have a drum lesson,' said Jesse. 'But I could do it tomorrow.'

Tracey looked disappointed. 'Well, maybe Adam and I can start on it this afternoon.'

Jesse shook his head angrily. 'That's not fair. It was my

idea, and if you and Adam get started without me, you'll plan it all.'

'We will not,' insisted Tracey.

'You will. You and Adam always do things like that. If we're going to work on this together, then we should all be in on it from the start.'

'Jesse's right,' added Tiffany. 'You and Adam usually do everything yourselves. This should be a group project if it's going to work at all.'

'All right, all right,' said Tracey. 'Let's not start a war about it. We'll do it during school. We can work on it in the Math-Science Club during free period, and we can ask about doing an assembly.'

Adam felt as if fate had intervened. The gods obviously wanted him to go on with his plan. Otherwise someone would have made sure that he didn't go to the mall that afternoon.

CHAPTER 11

ALISON AS A GUIDED MISSILE

Adam pushed Alison in her stroller across the acres of parking lot that surrounded the mall. Whenever he walked into the mall instead of being driven in, he felt like an alien. The mall wasn't made for people to walk to from the neighbourhood. It was made for cars, and it made pedestrians feel as if they were taking their lives in their hands if they dared to cross the icy and slippery parking lot. The cold made breathing hard.

As Adam glided Alison's stroller through the automatic doors into the mall, he felt the heat from the mall greet him like a welcoming host. The passageways of the mall were brightly lit. The vents above the hot bagel shop poured out the scent of freshly cooked dough into the air. Adam rolled Alison right under the vents, and she did just what he expected.

'Bagel!' she shouted.

'Does Alison want a bagel?' Adam asked.

Several people turned to smile at him, and Adam grinned back. He knew people thought it was cute to see a boy taking good care of his baby sister. He felt as if he were already in the role that he would have to play if he was going to pull this off. He wondered at how cool he felt. Did all thieves feel this calm?

Adam wheeled Alison into the bagel shop. 'One cinnamon raisin bagel,' Adam asked politely.

The girl behind the counter smiled at Adam.

'Just one?' she asked.

'Well, make it two,' said Adam.

'Your little brother is very cute.'

'Thanks,' said Adam. 'But she's a girl.'

Adam took the bagels and gave Alison one. He felt good, as if he were trying out a role and doing it perfectly. He was the nice boy, the one boy that you didn't have to worry about.

He wondered if people on drugs felt the way he did. He felt as if all his nerves were singing, as if he were going to bubble over. He wheeled Alison out into the middle of the mall. He passed J.C. Penny's and the shoe stores and the ice cream store and the video arcade. He could hear the sounds exploding from the video arcade. Then he realised that he was getting close to the electronics store. This was it. He looked inside. There was only one customer. Perfect.

He tried to tell himself that he didn't have to go through with it, but it was as if his mind was on automatic pilot. The plan almost had a life of its own. 'Don't do it,' whispered a voice in the back of his head. 'You don't want to be a thief.'

He ignored the voice and rolled Alison into the store. The saleslady looked up and seemed to recognise him. She smiled at him. Adam smiled back at her, wondering if she suspected anything. He told himself that he wouldn't do anything unless the opportunity was perfect. He would be careful. He would leave it up to fate.

He walked right past the chess computer, pretending that it didn't interest him at all. He went to the counter with the tape/clock radios. He found one just like Jesse's. He picked it up in his hand. Again, he was amazed at how tiny such a complicated machine could be. He checked to see if the machine had any heavy plastic tags on it. He knew those tags were rigged to set off an alarm if they were taken out of the store. There were no tags, except the price tag. $95.98. Adam's palms felt clammy, his stomach felt tied up into a tight ball, but the feeling of ultra-excitement remained.

He bent down and helped Alison out of her stroller. Alison looked a little amazed to be set free. She looked up at him as if not understanding. She waved her bagel in the air. She had only managed to take a few bites out of the side.

'Why we here?' asked Alison.

'Just looking,' said Adam. 'There's lots of things to play with in here.'

'I can touch?' asked Alison, obviously not believing that this store was different from others. Normally when they went into a store, Adam kept telling her not to touch anything.

'Sure,' said Adam, swallowing hard. He couldn't believe he was doing it. 'You're allowed to touch things in here.' He turned Alison around so that she faced the stereo display, which was tuned to a rock station. He felt like a bomber pilot releasing a guided missile.

Alison acted as if she had been programmed to help Adam become a thief. She made a beeline for the stereo system, just the way she would at home. Adam watched her.

Alison turned the knob just the way she loved to do at home. Suddenly an ear-shattering Keith Richards guitar line shattered the quiet of the store. The saleslady and the customer both covered their ears and stared at Alison.

Quicker than lightning, Adam slipped the tape/ clock radio into his knapsack and stuffed the knapsack into the pouch in Alison's stroller. He felt literally as if his heart was pounding at a thousand beats to the minute.

Alison bobbed up and down to the music. Adam ran toward her. 'Alison! Bad girl!' he shouted at her.

Alison stopped dancing and looked at him with shock. He had told her that this was a store where she could touch things. Adam scooped Alison up, put her firmly in the stroller, and strapped her in. He turned down the stereo. The saleslady was still staring at him.

'I'm so sorry,' Adam said in his most polite voice. 'I'll take her outside and out of your way.' Before Alison could start screaming, he wheeled her out of the store.

No alarms went off. He stood outside, and one of his legs wouldn't stop shaking. He had done it. The first step of his plan was completed. He had stolen the tape/clock radio. But he wished that his body would calm down. He felt as if it were taking him out of control. The excitement was so great that it scared him. The sensations were completely different from playing chess or Dungeons and Dragons. When he played chess, his mind worked as if it lived alone without a body. Stealing made him feel as if his mind had been blown away, leaving a sweating body in its cavity. The fear and excitement were so great that he couldn't imagine how anyone could steal all the time. Yet this plan had just begun. The clock radio was like a pawn in a chess game. It would have to be sacrificed.

CHAPTER 12

IN THE INTEREST OF SCIENCE

Adam raced past the stores as fast as he could. He wanted to be out of sight. Luckily the mall was so huge that he knew that he could disappear. At the very farthest end of the mall was the entrance to twin movie theatres. Adam wheeled Alison and her stroller full of stolen goods toward the movie theatres. Alison enjoyed the fast ride. She waved her bagel at people as she rolled by.

By the time they got to the theatres, Adam was drenched in sweat. There was a fake park outside the theatres, with plastic flowers surrounding it, and a plastic palm tree shading an old-fashioned park bench. He sat down and tried to catch his breath. He had done it. He had actually stolen a machine worth almost a hundred dollars.

He took out his pile of two-by-five cards and went through them to make sure they were in the right order. Although his hands were sweating, he was still proud of his plan. He knew that he could go back to the store right now and return the machine. He told himself that just because he had thought up the plan didn't mean he had to go through with it.

But stage one had gone perfectly. He owed it to himself to try stage two. After all, he didn't want the tape/clock

63

radio. He wanted the chess computer. And the chess computer was not out in the open in the store. He wouldn't have been able to steal it as easily as he had the clock radio. He needed the store to be empty if he were going to steal the chess computer.

Adam brushed his hair back. In some ways he knew that this next step would be the hardest. He was shy with strangers. But he had to go forward with the plan.

He stopped an older woman, dressed in a dark mink coat. Her hair was an unreal blue-grey colour, and it was perfectly combed. She had sharp brown eyes, but she looked nice.

'Excuse me,' said Adam, keeping his hands on Alison's stroller so that the stranger would know that he was a responsible boy helping to take care of his little sister.

The woman looked down at him suspiciously, clutching her pocketbook tightly to her side. Adam wished that people weren't so afraid of kids. 'Excuse me,' he repeated. 'But I'm working on a class project, and I wondered if you could just say one word into my tape recorder?'

'What's the word?' asked the woman, leaning away from him. Adam suspected she thought he was going to tell her a swear word.

At that moment Alison gave the woman one of her most beguiling smiles, a smile that made almost all adults melt.

'The word is *be*,' said Adam.

'*Bee*, the insect?'

'No, *be* the verb, like to exist.' Adam thought the woman would like it if he sounded intelligent. 'As I said, it's for a school project to discover what a sentence sounds like if strangers say each word.'

'It sounds like a very interesting project. Is it for English?'

'Behaviour science,' answered Adam, wondering whether it was going to take this long to get each word. Finally the woman shifted her purse from one hand to the other, still keeping it far out of Adam's reach. Adam pressed the red record button on his father's tape recorder.

The stolen machine was hidden in his knapsack. He handed the woman her card.

'Be!' said the woman into the tape recorder. She looked at the machine as if expecting it to applaud.

'Thank you,' said Adam.

'Is that all?' the woman asked. She sounded disappointed. Adam wondered whether this was the most exciting thing that had happened to her all day. If it was, he felt very sorry for her.

Adam worked for an hour, stopping people and asking them to speak just one word into his tape recorder. He was surprised by how many people seemed frightened by a kid. Often he had to change his story.

Alison became increasingly fidgety as time wore on. She stopped being a help, and the whole project was becoming too much like work. Adam wished that he had never started it. He bought Alison a candy bar to keep her quiet.

'You know, I'm likely to go through my whole allowance,' muttered Adam. 'Here I steal a hundred-dollar machine, and I barely have enough money to keep my baby sister in candy bars.'

'Bagel!' demanded Alison, holding out her hand.

'Candy bar,' said Adam, unwrapping it for her. He thumbed through his index cards. He was almost finished, but his next word would be tough. He needed someone to say the word *bathroom*.

He looked around to see if he could find someone who wouldn't be embarrassed. He stopped a kid wearing a Buffalo Bills football jacket. The kid looked as if he were about Adam's age.

'Excuse me,' said Adam. 'Can you help me out?'

The kid looked Adam up and down. 'You looking for a handout? A kid from St Luke's? That's a rich one, a kid from St Luke's begging. Hey, that's a pun. Do you get it? A "rich one".'

Adam felt sick to his stomach. He had forgotten that he had on his St Luke's blazer. 'Stupid! Stupid!' he thought to himself. He was a lousy thief. What kind of thief wore his school blazer to steal? He was an idiot. He took off his jacket and stuffed it behind the stolen clock radio. Sweat had soaked through his shirt, making huge wet circles under his arms.

'Well, what do you want?' the kid asked impatiently.

'I need your voice,' said Adam. 'You have to say just one word into my tape recorder. It's for a project in behavioural science.'

'Yeah? What kind of behaviour?'

'I just need you to say the word *bathroom* into my tape recorder.'

The kid started laughing so hard that Alison looked up at him and started to laugh with him. 'What are you, some kind of kid pervert?'

'No,' said Adam. 'It's in the interest of science. I'm studying the different ways people say *bathroom*. Some people get very defensive. They can barely whisper it.' Adam wanted the kid to think that saying the word *bathroom* would be a challenge.

He held the tape recorder to the kid. The kid acted as if he were about to appear on TV. He patted his hair to make sure it was in place and straightened his shoulders.

'Okay,' said Adam. 'When I push the red button, you say *bathroom*.'

'BATHROOM!'

The kid's voice bounced off the roof of the mall and several strangers gave them filthy looks.

'How did I do?' asked the kid.

'Great,' said Adam. 'Thanks.'

Adam waited for the kid to leave, but the kid seemed to be in no hurry.

'I'm Chuckie Mevis,' said the kid. He stuck out his hand.

Adam tried to think quickly. He couldn't give Chuckie his real name.

'I'm Sebastian,' Adam said quickly, remembering with relief the name Tracey had given him.

'Who is the next patsy you're gonna ask to say *bathroom*? I figure I'll stick around and watch the next guy make a fool of himself.'

Before Adam could say anything, Chuckie pointed to a good-looking teenager in a purple jumpsuit. The girl had long blonde hair that she wore loose. 'Want me to get her for you?' asked Chuckie.

Before Adam could answer, Chuckie jumped up and ran to the girl in the jumpsuit. Adam could see Chuckie pointing to him. As they got closer, Chuckie was saying, 'And you will be a star. You will star in an exclusive St Luke's production. Isn't that high class?'

Adam wished with all his heart that he hadn't worn his blazer. He felt so stupid. Suddenly, he wanted the whole thing to be over. He was exhausted. He decided to see if he could finish it in one sweep.

The girl was smiling at Chuckie even though he was about three years younger than she was. 'Okay, what's this all about?' she asked.

'I need you to say *lock the door*,' said Adam.

Chuckie stared at him. 'What happened to *bathroom*?' he whispered.

'We ask the girls to say *lock the door*,' Adam whispered hastily. He added a wink.

Chuckie winked back as if he understood. He gave the girl one of the most charming smiles Adam had ever seen. Adam knew that he could be charming when he needed to be, but watching Chuckie made him feel like an amateur.

'I hope this isn't going to be used for the soundtrack for a porno flick,' asked the girl.

Adam felt his face get all hot. He wished he could control his blushing.

The girl turned to Chuckie. 'Your friend is cute when he turns all red.' Adam felt himself turning an even deeper shade of red.

'Turn the machine on,' urged Chuckie.

Adam felt as if Chuckie had taken control. He pressed the record button.

'Lock the door!' said the girl in a clear, low voice that made her sound even older than she looked.

Chuckie smiled at her. 'My friend and I thank you,' he said.

Adam put the tape recorder back in his bag. He now had the entire message. He heard the tape recorder knock against the stolen clock radio. Now he had to get rid of Chuckie.

He turned to Chuckie and stuck out his hand. 'I want to thank you,' said Adam, sounding pompous to himself. He hoped Chuckie would get the point and get lost.

'You all done?'

'Yeah, as I said, thanks.'

'You gonna listen to it all now?' asked Chuckie.

'No, I've got to anlayse it,' said Adam. 'I'll do it at home.'

'Where's your home?' Chuckie asked.

Adam felt trapped. It was bad enough that Chuckie knew where he went to school. He couldn't allow him to know where he lived.

'I'm not allowed to tell,' said Adam.

Chuckie took a step back. 'Excuse me,' he said in an exaggerated voice. 'I forgot kids from St Luke's have to be so careful. You wouldn't want to play with anyone who wasn't rich like you.'

Then Chuckie walked away without another word. Adam watched him go. He had got rid of him, all right, but Adam felt sick to his stomach.

CHAPTER 13

A TALKING TIME BOMB

Adam watched Chuckie's back. He imagined himself calling after him and saying, 'Wait, Chuckie. I'm not a rich snob, I'm a thief.'

Alison was sound alseep in her stroller. Adam wished that she would wake up and scream, anything to stop him from taking the next step. But she slept on.

The late-afternoon movie crowd, mostly old people with just a few kids, was lining up at the twin theatres. Adam needed a private place. Now was the tricky part. He had to take the tape he had just made and put it in the stolen clock radio.

Adam spotted a sign with a stick figure of a man. He remembered the girl at the bagel counter calling Alison a boy. He could wheel Alison in there and make the change in a toilet stall. Somehow it felt appropriate. Adam remembered seeing lots of spy movies on television in which the bad guy fixed his equipment in a john. But Adam had never believed that he would be the bad guy.

The men's room was empty, and Adam was grateful. Quickly he locked himself in a stall. He ejected the tape from his father's tape recorder and took the stolen merchandise out of his knapsack. He held the little tape/clock radio in his hand. He fumbled as he tried to push his own tape (the one with the message of the thousand voices) into the machine. It bounced back at him. Adam took a deep breath and tried again. This time he heard the satisfying click as the tape settled into the correct position.

Adam looked at his watch. 4:22 PM. If he set the clock for 4:15 PM, it wouldn't go off until the next afternoon. He would have a whole day to breathe, to be away from the mall. He felt as if the mall had become his prison. Originally, Adam had hoped to accomplish the whole caper in one day, but now he realized it was unrealistic. More than anything, he wanted to get out of the mall. He needed fresh air.

He set the clock for 4:15 PM. That would give him twenty-four hours.

Then he wheeled Alison out of the men's room. He put the clock radio back into the pouch behind Alison's stroller and walked purposefully the whole length of the mall, back to the computer store.

The computer store was empty of customers. The saleslady was sitting at the console of a computer, typing in a program. She stopped and stood up.

'Hi again,' she said. 'You're getting to a regular customer.'

'Not customer,' said Adam. 'I've come to confess.'

The saleslady did a double take. 'Confess?'

Adam reached into the pouch and took out the stolen tape/clock radio and handed it to her.

'Actually, it's my baby sister who should confess. She's the one who took it.'

The saleslady looked down at Alison, sleeping in her stroller. Her little hands hung limply out from her sides, and her mouth was slightly open. 'She looks a little young for a thief.'

'I'm sure she didn't mean to take it,' said Adam. 'But I found it in her stroller. I think she grabbed it. I brought it back as soon as I could.' Adam willed his voice to sound as sincere as he could. He wanted to look embarrassed, and it wasn't hard. Alison had not innocently grabbed the clock radio. Adam had stolen it, and now he was placing it back, like a time bomb. Adam corrected himself. It wasn't like a time bomb, it *was* a time bomb – a talking time bomb.

The woman took the clock radio from him and put it back on the shelf. 'Thanks for returning it. A lot of kids wouldn't have bothered. You were in here before with your older sister. Where's she?'

Adam almost said, 'What older sister' when he remembered Tracey's lie. 'Oh, she had a piano lesson,' he lied easily. Lies piled on lies so quickly that Adam felt as if he were being buried under an avalanche of lies.

Luckily, once again, Alison saved the day. She woke up and started to cry. 'I have to get my baby sister home,' Adam said quickly. 'She's probably hungry. I'm real sorry again about her wandering off with your merchandise. She's not a thief.'

'Of course not,' said the saleslady. 'You were terrific to return it. I owe you one. Your name is Sebastian, isn't it?'

Adam almost said no. More and more he realised that being a thief was a lot trickier than he had imagined. The things that made him good at games, like his wonderful memory, turned out to be faulty tools. It was as if he had picked up a nice heavy hammer and found out that the hammer's head was loose.

'My name's Vanessa,' said the saleswoman, sticking out her hand. Adam shook her hand. 'What's your name, sweetie?' asked Vanessa, talking in a babyish accent. She crouched down next to Alison.

'Alison,' said Alison, enunciating each syllable distinctly. Adam felt as if each syllable was a gate slamming him into jail. Somehow they'd be able to trace him because Alison gave her real name. He held his breath, hoping that Alison wouldn't give their last name.

'Well, Alison,' said Vanessa, 'you've got to learn not to take things that don't belong to you. You won't always have your big brother around to make sure you don't get in

71

trouble.'

Vanessa stood up. She held her hand out again for Adam to shake. 'I want to thank you again. They probably would have taken that loss out of my salary. Come back when you have some more time. I'll let you do some demonstration programs. You can play Pac-Man or Galaxian ... whatever.'

'I'm not good at those video games,' stammered Adam.

'Well, then you can learn some simple programming. Basic, Cobol, Fortran.'

'Apples and worms,' said Adam, pleased that he knew the slang for the different languages that different computers took.

'It's the language of the future,' said Vanessa, smiling at him.

Adam felt tears in the corners of his eyes. 'Oh, no,' he thought to himself. He wanted to throw himself on Vanessa's lap and tell her the whole plot. He felt as if he were going crazy. He wanted to be out of the store, but it was as if his feet were nailed to the floor, as if suddenly he couldn't move anymore. His body was no longer connected to his mind. Vanessa was still holding his hand, and Adam felt as if she were going to keep it, that he would never get it back.

Finally, Alison cried again. 'I've really got to get her home,' Adam said, feeling as if he were coming out of a trance. Vanessa dropped his hand.

'I just wanted you to know, I think you're a real special kid for returning that clock radio,' she said. 'You know, it's our most expensive model because it comes with a tape deck in it. You can program it to wake you up with your favourite tapes.'

'Oh, really?' said Adam as innocently as he could. 'I didn't notice. I thought it was just a plain clock radio. Well, good-bye.'

Adam wheeled Alison out the door. Vanessa waved to him. Adam laughed to himself. He felt good about that last exchange. He was proud of himself for pretending that he hadn't realised the clock radio played tapes. It was an excellent lie. Perhaps he wasn't such a bad thief after all. First of all, he had stolen the most expensive clock radio in the store. Then he had returned it. 'Vanessa would never suspect me,' he repeated to himself. The plan was a great one.

CHAPTER 14

DOOMSDAY ISN'T SUPPOSED TO BE FUN

At two in the afternoon, free period, Adam went down to the Math-Science Club. He was worried. If the doomsday scenario took too long, he wouldn't make it back to the mall on time. He decided that at three o'clock, he'd just have to think of an excuse to leave.

When he got there, he discovered that Tracey had bought huge sheets of graph paper. 'I thought we'd graph it out first, then we can figure out where to put it.'

'I thnk we should use the whole school grounds,' said Tiffany. 'We could make the Great Hall ground zero. People will either die instantly or slowly, and we'll decide it by a roll of the dice.'

'Treasure will be water and food,' said Jesse. 'This is such an excellent idea. Who knows? Maybe we can sell it and make a lot of money.'

'I thought you weren't supposed to make money out of disarmament,' said Adam sourly.

'It wouldn't be wrong if it were for a good cause,' said Tracey. 'Besides, we could donate the money to a group that's working for peace. You'd do that, wouldn't you, Jesse?'

Jesse seemed surprised to find Tracey on his side. He

nodded.

Adam couldn't concentrate on the Big Bomb or on their graph. All he could do was to daydream about what would happen if the world ended. If an atomic bomb fell on Buffalo before 4:15 PM, a direct hit on the mall, all of Adam's problems would be over. He'd be dead, of course, and so would his parents and Alison, but the clock radio with the tape in it would also disintegrate.

'Adam,' said Tracey sharply. 'If you didn't want to help, why did you say you would?'

'You made me, remember?' Adam regretted his tone of voice.

'You stink, Adam,' said Tracey quickly. 'Don't you care if the world blows up?'

'No,' said Adam. He looked Tracey in the eye.

Tracey stared at him.

'I'll go home,' said Adam, secretly glad that they were having a fight. Now he had an excuse to leave.

'Are you sick?' Tracey asked.

Adam shook his head. 'I'm okay. I'm sorry I haven't been much fun to be with.' Adam could hear the whine in his voice, and he hated it.

'Doomsday isn't supposed to be fun,' snapped Tracey.

'Hey, you know, that's not a bad title,' said Tiffany, obviously trying to smooth things over. 'We can make a big banner. "Doomsday isn't supposed to be fun!"'

'It's great,' said Tracey, but she didn't sound as if she meant it. 'Come on, Adam, let's not fight. We've got to stick together.'

Jesse held a black cutout of a bomb in his hand. He put it on the graph. 'Do you think we should put the stockpile under the football field, or someplace else?'

'Someplace else,' said Tracey, turning away from Adam and crouching down on all fours so she could study the graph.

Adam held one of the bomb cutouts in his hand. He couldn't think of where to put it. 'Do you kids ever think this whole thing is stupid?' he asked.

'You mean Doomsday Dungeons and Dragons?' asked Tracey. 'Sure, some kids might call it stupid, but we have to risk it. I don't want to die before I'm sixteen. We've got to do something.'

'That wasn't what I was talking about' said Adam. 'I wasn't talking about this idea. I think it's pretty clever.'

'Thanks,' said Jesse. He grinned.

Adam wanted to let his friends know what he meant. Suddenly he felt it was important that they understand. 'What's the point of anything?' asked Adam. 'The odds are that we won't live to grow up. We'll be disintegrated by an Atomic War.'

'I know,' said Jesse. 'It really burns me up.' He giggled.

'It's not a joke,' said Tracey.

'I know what Adam's talking about,' said Tiffany. 'Like, why do your homework or clean up your room if the bomb might drop at any minute?'

'Sort of,' said Adam. He longed to be like Tiffany. Her life sounded so simple. Imagine feeling that the worst thing was not cleaning up your room. He wondered what his friends would think if they knew he was well on his way to stealing a $400 chess computer. They would be horrified, he knew.

'Lots of kids have nightmares about Atomic War and the end of the world,' said Tiffany. 'Are you having nightmares?'

Adam shook his head impatiently. 'No, I'm not having nightmares about the bomb. You sound like a shrink. Come on, let's talk about something else.'

'See,' said Tracey triumphantly. 'You're like a lot of kids – you don't want to talk about Atomic War because it's upsetting. But if it's upsetting, we should do something about it.'

'Hey, nobody asked you to give a lecture. Save it for the assembly,' snapped Adam.

Tracey looked as if she wanted to hit him. 'I'm sorry,' said Adam. 'I guess I'm tired or something. Come on, you and I never fight.'

'Well, we're certainly fighting now,' said Tracey. 'I wasn't lecturing you, and I'm sorry if you're bored. I expect you to care about things. Maybe other kids think I'm boring because I talk about issues, but not you, you're different.'

Tiffany and Jesse stared down at the graph paper, as if wishing they were somewhere else. Adam felt furious, so angry that he actually did feel like slapping Tracey. He wanted to kill her *'Why?'* he shouted. *'Why am I so different?'* he was screaming.

'Because you used to be nice!' shouted Tracey at the top of her lungs.

'Terrific,' said Adam, lowering his voice. He felt defeated. 'Let's hear it for nice. I can just see it on my tombstone. "He was a nice boy."'

'Maybe you *should* go home,' said Tracey. She had lowered her voice, too, but she sounded as if she hated him. 'I don't think you have to worry about being too nice. That's not one of your problems anymore.'

Adam felt confused. He didn't understand how they had got into such a terrible fight so quickly. 'I don't understand,' he said softly. 'I don't understand what we're fighting about.'

'I don't either,' said Tracey. 'But you make me mad. You act like you don't care about anything.'

'Maybe it's just the bomb,' said Adam. 'Maybe Tiffany was right. Maybe I just can't take the pressure of thinking that the world could blow up tomorrow. It makes me crazy.'

Tracey lost the look of absolute fury. Her face softened. 'You can't let the bomb take over your life,' she said. 'We've just got to do what we can to make sure that the people in power hear us.'

'I can't help it,' said Adam. 'I feel so crazy when I realise our lives could be blown away at any second.' Adam hated himself as he talked. Jesse and Tiffany nodded their heads in agreement. 'You're right. Maybe I'm just too upset to work on it now.'

Adam looked at his watch. Three o'clock. School was officially out, and he had plenty of time to get to the mall.

Tracey was his best friend. He was deceiving her about his feelings. It felt even worse than lying. He knew she was a sucker for any talk about Atomic War and bombs. He was playing on her feelings. Adam knew that the bomb wasn't making him crazy. He was stealing the chess computer because he wanted it, because his friends were all richer than he was.

Adam knew that he wasn't crazy, but he knew also that he wasn't a nice boy. Nice boys don't steal.

CHAPTER 15

A ROBBERY IN
PROGRESS

Adam was breathless by the time he reached the mall. He stepped on the rubber mat, and the doors to the mall opened as if for a king. He felt so excited that he imagined he was giving off rays of energy. His eyesight felt unnaturally keen, his hearing sharp.

He glanced down at his watch. 3:48. He had made it from school in plenty of time. He felt like jumping and spinning. It wasn't just nerves. He felt a surge of power. In just a little while, his message would go off. He would know if his plan worked. Vanessa would hear:

BEWARE. YOU WILL BE HURT
IF YOU DO NOT DO AS I SAY.
GO TO THE BATHROOM AND
LOCK THE DOOR.

She wouldn't know where the voice was coming from, and she would never know *who* was speaking. That was the glory of his plan, so many voices on the tape. The police would think that a gang was involved. They'd never guess it was just one little kid.

He walked by the computer store and saw Vanessa

inside, standing with her back to him. He breathed a sigh of relief because the store was empty. If there were customers, the whole plot could fall apart. But the store was empty. Adam felt as if the powers that controlled the universe wanted him to succeed. They were helping him to steal.

He stood behind a pillar in the centre of the mall. The pillar had a map on it that said, YOU ARE HERE. Adam licked his lips. 'That's right,' he thought. 'You are here. You are actually going to steal a chess computer. In a few minutes it will be yours.'

His entire insides felt as if they were racing, like a powerful drug had been injected into his body. He couldn't keep still. He peeked around the pillar to look into the computer store, but he was scared Vanessa would catch a glimpse of him. He glanced back down at his watch: 4:10.

Suddenly his mood changed like a misfired rocket, exploding in midair. He was scared. He wanted to race into the store and tear the tape from the clock radio. He wanted to make time stand still. He was too young to risk going to jail.

Adam imagined himself before a judge saying, 'Well, sir, I just wanted a talking chess machine, and we couldn't afford it.' The judge would think he was a spoiled brat. He would throw the book at him. It wasn't like Adam was stealing bread, stealing something that he needed to live.

If he were caught, he would probably never go to college, never lead a normal life. He might never get married. Who would want to marry someone who had been in jail? He would never get to see the world. More than anything Adam wanted to go to Africa to see wild animals in game preserves. If he were caught and thrown in jail, he would never get there.

'Hold it,' Adam said to himself. 'You're being crazy. It's not such a big deal. Millions of kids steal. Besides, who says you'll get caught?'

Within seconds his mood swung again. Once more he

felt ██████████████████████, even more powerful than before. He *knew*, just *knew* his plan was going to work. It was brilliant. Soon he would have his very own chess computer. It would be *his*. It was so simple. He wanted the chess computer, yes, *needed* it! He needed it if he were going to become a great chess player.

4:15. The tape was running.

Adam held his breath. He peered around the pillar and glanced into the computer store. He couldn't see Vanessa. He stepped from behind the pillar and faced the glass doors of the computer store. It looked empty. Vanessa was locked in the bathroom. His plan was working.

He felt a surge of power. He saw the sign over the chess machine, written in glitter letters: CHALLENGE THE CHAMPION.

'I am the champion,' thought Adam to himself. Quickly he picked up the chess machine. It was hardly bigger than the tape/clock radio. It fit easily into his knapsack.

Then he walked out of the computer store. He put the knapsack on his back. He looked at his watch. It had taken him less than ten seconds to steal the chess computer.

He passed a bank of public telephones and paused. Now that the robbery was over, he thought about Vanessa. Was she crouched in the bathroom believing she would be killed? Adam liked her. She had been nice to him.

He dashed into the phone booth and dialled 911. Then he took off his sweater and pulled it across the receiver. 'I'd like to report a robbery in progress,' he whispered in a low voice.

'*What? Speak up!*' said the voice at the other end of the line. She sounded annoyed.

'A robbery in progress!' whispered Adam hoarsely. 'At the computer store at the Hillsdale Mall!' Adam felt as if he were shouting and whispering at the same time.

'*Who is this?*' demanded the voice.

Adam slammed the phone down. The receiver was wet and slippery from the sweat on his hands. Adam rubbed his hands on his pants.

He hurried out of the ████████████████ ██t he had even bothered to call. He remembered reading that shoplifting was not a crime until you actually left the premises of the store. Did that apply to the mall? Was he technically not a thief until he stepped out into real air?

Adam stepped on the mat in front of the automatic doors. The doors parted. He felt the blast of cold air. He walked. *Now* he was a thief.

The wind blew sharp and cold. Although it was before 4:30 PM, the cars had their headlights on as they turned into the mall. Snow was lightly falling, and Adam could see the flakes reflected in headlights.

What if he fell under the wheels of one of the cars? The police would find the crushed chess computer under his broken body. His parents would know he was a thief. But he would be dead, he wouldn't have to worry about it.

Adam realised that he didn't have to wait for an accident to happen. He could throw himself under one of the cars. His breath came in gasps. He had never thought about suicide before. He saw himself bloody under a car's wheels. He wondered whether the silicon microchips in the Chess Challenger would survive. Maybe the voice in the machine would keep going, eerily chanting out, 'Knight to bishop three.' The computer's voice would live, but Adam's own voice would be stilled forever.

Adam wondered exactly how to throw himself under a car. He would have to do it so that he would be sure he would be killed. It would be awful if all that happened was that he broke a leg. A broken leg wouldn't do him any good. He would have to be dead. But he wanted it to look like an accident. He'd have to try to throw himself headfirst so that his head would get crushed. After all, it was his head that got him into all this trouble in the first place.

Adam came to the end of the parking lot. Now he had to cross the highway to get to his house. The thickening snow made the road slippery. Adam watched cars, moving slowly now because of the snow.

He waited on the corner for the light to turn green and then he crossed. Halfway across the highway it struck him. A boy about to kill himself would not cross the highway with a green light. Adam knew he wasn't going to kill himself.

He made it safely to the other side. He turned around and looked at the cars streaming by. He felt relieved, idiotically glad that he hadn't fallen under the tyres of a car. The Chess Challenger was still on his back. Maybe when he got home he would play it alone in his room. After all, that was why he had stolen it in the first place.

CHAPTER 16

STEALING TRUST

Adam hid the Chess Challenger in an old box that used to hold his Monopoly game. It fit perfectly. He put the Monopoly board and all the hotels and houses in a brown bag. Then he put Scotch tape around the edges of the Monopoly box, just in case his mother or father should happen to pick it up. Then he put the stolen machine in the back of his closet.

He waited for his parents to come home. The house seemed so silent. He wanted to take the Chess Challenger out and play with it, but he was afraid.

He didn't look at the Chess Challenge for twenty-four hours. He had no time alone in the house, and he was afraid to play with it when his parents were home. However, the next night, Adam's parents had a teacher's meeting, and Adam offered to baby-sit. Tracey and Jesse wanted him to work on their doomsday scenario, but Adam told them he couldn't. He wanted to be alone with his stolen machine.

He waited until Alison was asleep before he slit the Scotch tape on his Monopoly box and took out the Chess Challenger. He held it in his hand, and his hand shook a little. It was hard to believe that only twenty-four hours ago he had stolen the machine. It felt so long ago, as if it were something he had done years before.

Adam set up the chess pieces on the chess machine's sensory board. He set the challenger at the beginner's level. Adam took white. He moved his white pawn. The machine's lights blinked, and then the mechanical voice came out of the machine's microphone. 'King's pawn to bishop three.' Adam moved the machine's pawn. He watched the digital clock on the machine's control panel flip the seconds. Soon the machine said, 'You have twenty seconds to make your move.'

Adam moved his knight.

The machine beat him in six more moves. Adam stared at the board in amazement. He shouldn't have lost that game. He felt angry, as if the machine were a person who had wanted to crush his ego. He set up the pieces again.

The machine beat him again, and again, and again. In fact, it beat Adam five times in a row before Adam won a game. Adam was disgusted with himself. He pushed the machine up a level. He decided that as long as he was going to be beaten, he might as well be beaten at the championship level.

Ironically, as soon as the machine began making more complicated moves, Adam's mind switched into high gear. He got involved in the game. The machine wasn't beating him. Adam knew that he wasn't winning, but he wasn't losing either. He felt that he might get a draw. 'I'm not such a pushover, am I?' he said to the machine, as if the machine were a real person with a personality. Adam concentrated with all his might.

He concentrated so hard that he almost missed the sound of his parents' car pulling into the driveway. As soon as he heard it he stopped the game right away and put it back into the Monopoly box. He didn't think he had time to get the box into the closet, so he shoved it under the bed. He turned out his lights.

Within seconds, he heard his father's footsteps. Adam heard his father open the door to Alison's room. Then he heard Alison's door close, and he knew his father would come into his room, the way that he had ever since Adam was a baby.

Adam turned his head to the wall. Suddenly he felt tears in his eyes, and he knew he was going to cry. He felt so embarrassed, he wanted to die. He tried to make his breath come evenly so that his father would think he was sleeping.

Adam heard his own door open. His father tiptoed in. 'Adam,' he whispered. 'Come on, Adam, I know you're awake. I saw you turn off your light as we drove into the driveway.' His father's voice had a teasing quality to it. Adam knew that he wasn't mad at him for still being awake.

His father sat down on the edge of the bed and rested his hand on Adam's shoulder. Adam rolled over, rubbing his eyes as if pretending just to wake up. His father laughed.

'Come on, Adam. What's going on?' asked his father. 'Why the big charade? Was Alison so terrible that you didn't want to talk to us about it?'

'No, she was fine,' said Adam, rubbing his eyes, hoping his father wouldn't be able to tell that he had been crying just seconds before. 'I just happened to turn my light out just as you came home. I didn't hear you come in.'

Adam's father looked as if he didn't believe him.

'You know, your mom and I really appreciate the way you help out around here. It would be tough on us if we had to pay for baby-sitters right now.'

'I know, Dad. I don't mind.'

Adam's father kept his hand on Adam's shoulder. It felt strange. They didn't touch much anymore. Adam felt that he had to resist the temptation to put his head on his father's chest and to feel his father's arms holding him tight.

His father took his free hand and gently lifted the hair from Adam's forehead. He leaned forward to kiss Adam on the forehead. He stopped. 'You look like you've been crying. What's wrong?'

Adam rubbed his eyes. 'No ... No ... it's just something got in my eye before ...' Adam stammered.

'Adam ...' His father paused. 'You look worried ... What's bothering you? Is it all this talk about nuclear war? I think it's terrific that you're designing a Dungeons and Dragons doomsday game. I think it will really teach some kids, make them think about things in a new way.'

Adam snorted a laugh before he could stop himself. He shook his head quickly. 'I'm sorry, Dad, I didn't mean to laugh. Sure the bomb scared me, but ...'

'But what? Something's been on your mind these last few days. Are you still thinking about the lie about skiing? You can rest easy. I talked to your mom about it. I confessed that I did know how to ski. She laughed at me. Maybe we'll all try it one afternoon.'

'What about it being too expensive?' asked Adam.

'I think it is, but we'll work it out. We can at least try it.'

Adam didn't say anything.

'Don't you think that's a good idea?' his father asked.

Adam turned his face away. 'I don't deserve it,' he muttered.

His father put his hand on Adam's chin and forced him to look at him. 'What the hell are you talking about?' he asked. 'Of course you deserve it. Are you making a liar out of me again? I just told you how much mom and I appreciate you.'   Adam could feel the tears in his eyes. 'Dad, I don't deserve it. I stole something.'

Adam could see the shock register on his father's face. 'What?'

Adam swallowed. He looked at his father's face, which just a moment ago had looked so soft and loving. Now his eyes looked angry, his mouth was set. Adam tried to meet his father's eyes, but he couldn't. His stomach felt as if it were turning over. He knew he couldn't tell his father that he had stolen an expensive chess computer.

'What did you steal?' Adam's father asked. 'Adam, answer me.'

'I stole a candy bar,' whispered Adam.

Adam's father blinked. 'A candy bar? You don't even like candy.'

'I know it was a crazy thing to do, but some kids at school were talking about how they like to steal things from department stores and I felt like such a goody-goody because I had never stolen, that I decided to try it. But I hated it.'

'Which kids steal from department stores?' asked Adam's father.

Adam stared at his father. 'Dad, I can't tell. Come on ...'

Adam's father shook his head. 'You're right. I'm sorry I asked you. Adam, look. I know some kids think stealing is a game. But it's not. Look at me. You know, I don't usually lecture you, but I hate kids who steal ... anything, even a candy bar. Stealing isn't wrong just because it's against the law. Some laws are stupid and some laws are unfair. But not the law against stealing. The Bible uses just four simple words. 'You shall not steal.' They are probably the most simple and most important words in the Bible. The only words more important are "You shall not kill."'

Adam's father paused. He seemed embarrassed to be lecturing, but he sounded so sincere. Adam knew that his father meant every word he was saying. 'You see, Adam, if people want to live together they have to trust each other. Every time someone steals from someone, he or she doesn't just steal a TV or a piece of jewellery or a sweater or a candy bar, you steal trust. When you stole that candy bar, you didn't just steal the money the owner of the store paid to buy that candy bar, you told your victim, "Don't trust other people." It's worse when a child steals because you're saying, "Don't trust children. Don't trust the generation behind you." People want to trust children because they want to believe the future will be better than today, so that when you steal, you steal hope and you steal trust. Every time you steal, you're announcing to the world that people can't live together in peace. Do you understand what I'm talking about?'

Adam wanted to sob. He could imagine his father's rage if he found out his own son was a *real* thief, not just a boy who had snitched a candy bar. 'You steal hope, and you steal trust.' His own father would never trust him again. Adam felt as if he were turning into lead. He remembered the surge of energy in the mall. Now he hated that feeling, hated himself. He recalled the moment when he wanted to race into the computer store and tear the tape out of the clock radio. If only he had followed his conscience then.

'Adam?' asked his father slowly. 'Tell me what you're thinking.'

Adam closed his eyes for a second. He couldn't, *couldn't* tell his father what he was thinking. His father thought he stole a lousy candy bar. He just couldn't tell him the truth, tell his father that he, Adam, could never be trusted.

'What should my punishment be?' Adam asked, his voice cracked.

'Punishment. I don't know. What do you think your punishment should be?'

Adam just shook his head back and forth.

'You think about it. You know, your mom and I aren't big on punishment with a capital P. We want you to know right from wrong. Personally, if you felt bad enough to tell me about it, I think maybe you've almost been punished enough.'

Adam swallowed hard. He couldn't begin to tell his father how bad he felt. 'Adam, look,' said his father. 'Neither Mom or I expect you to be perfect, you know. Sometimes I think you're harder on yourself than you need to be. It's just that I meant every word I said about stealing. I hate stealing. I hate kids who steal, especially kids like you who aren't starving. I know we can't buy you all the things that your friends have, but Mom and I have always hoped that we've given you much more than just things. We love you. We want you to grow up to care for the important things in life, other people, ideas. Both your mom and I love the work we do, even if we don't get paid very much for it. I love teaching young kids, and I'm good at it. Your mom is terrific at getting kids to love reading. There's so much more to life than just buying the latest gadget or fad. You get a new game and then it sits in the closet.' Adam's father smiled. 'There's even more to life than skiing.'

'Does my telling you that I stole mean that we won't go skiing?'

Adam's father shook his head. 'Look, stealing a candy bar is not a capital offence. I'm glad you told me, and I think you won't do it again. I'd rather you think about what I said to you than worry about your punishment.'

Adam felt as if he were sinking into quicksand. The truth was so much worse – that he had stolen something worth hundreds of dollars, and he knew that he could go to jail or a juvenile detention home for what he had done.

Adam's father got up off the bed and straightened out Adam's blanket, just the way he used to do when Adam was really young. Then he left the room. Adam wanted to burst into tears. He buried his face in his pillow, and tears came streaming out of his eyes. He felt like a crying machine. He drew the pillow closer to muffle the sound of his crying. He hated himself, hated that he was now the type of kid who could steal, the type of kid who couldn't be trusted. He had stolen the machine to be like Jesse and Tracey, but it wasn't working. He just felt more different. He couldn't even show them the machine for fear that they might mention it to his parents. He would never be like Jesse and Tracey. He would never have as much money as they had, and now he would never be like them because he was a thief.

Stealing the chess machine was nothing like a Dungeons and Dragons game. In Dungeons and Dragons, if Adam's character got trapped in a cave, Adam could always roll the dice and make up another character.

Adam realised that he couldn't change his character with a roll of the dice. Nothing was going to change the fact that now he was a thief.

Right now, Adam couldn't even remember why he had

wanted the stupid chess machine so much. His parents weren't rich, but he wouldn't trade them for Tracey's parents of Jesse's mother, or for anyone.

Yet hidden in the Monopoly box under his bed was the machine that he had stolen. It was like a monster, and it could beat him easily at chess.

Adam was the best chess player he knew. Yet the machine beat him as if he were a lightweight. Adam hated the machine. But what could he do with it? He couldn't take it back. If he turned himself in, Vanessa would call the police. Adam couldn't face going to jail. He couldn't face telling his parents that he actually had stolen a four-hundred-dollar machine. So he was stuck with the machine. Adam imagined himself being buried someday and the machine being placed in his coffin.

CHAPTER 17

WHAT'S THIS?
ONE YOU STOLE?

For the next week at school, they worked hard on the doomsday scenario. They decided that as many as fifty kids would play at one time. Each player would roll the dice to determine how far away he or she lived from ground zero. At ground zero a one-megaton bomb would fall. This is one of the smallest bombs in the Soviet Union's arsenal, but it has eighty times the strength of the bomb that fell on Hiroshima.

Jesse argued that it should be a twenty-megaton bomb because that was the Soviet Union's most popular bomb. They have at least 113 twenty-megaton bombs. But Tracey and Tiffany argued that a twenty-megaton bomb ruined the game. The mushroom cloud would be seventy miles. Buffalo, its subrubs, and Lake Erie would be turned into a flat, scorched desert in just a few seconds. They would all just disappear in radioactive dust, to fall wherever the wind was blowing.

So they decided on a one-megaton bomb, which would flatten an area of sixty-one square miles. Buildings would fall on people in an area of one hundred square miles. A roll of the dice would determine whether you were caught in the fireball and killed instantly or injured in an outlying area.

Some people would be survivors. They would have to run away from their families and friends, and they would die more slowly from radiation or starvation.

They used calculators to figure out the odds. It was gruesome. Tracey had found a book of stories of survivors of Hiroshima, and she and Jesse took turns reading from it.

Kinzo Nishida recalls, 'While taking my severely wounded wife out to the riverbank by the side of the hill of Nakahiro-machi, I was horrified, indeed, at the sight of a stark-naked man standing in the rain with his eyeball in his palm. He seemed to be in great pain, but there was nothing I could do for him,' read Tracey.

'That's disgusting,' said Adam.

'But it will make it come alive,' said Tracey. 'I think that with a roll of the dice you have to come upon a man with his eyeball in his hand and try to help him.'

'That's terrific,' said Jesse. 'It will be like a horrible treasure hunt. The survivors will keep coming upon one horror after another.'

'I have one for the survivors,' said Tiffany. 'Somebody should be pregnant.'

'Great,' said Adam. 'Pregnant when the bomb is dropped.'

'I mean it,' said Tiffany. 'Someone will roll the dice and their character will be a pregnant woman. In Hiroshima after the bomb, all these babies were born with tiny heads and they were retards . . . so with a roll of a dice you survive, but you have to try to take care of a mentally retarded baby.'

Adam felt like being sick to his stomach. He stood up. The whole school was talking about the Dungeons and Dragons doomsday scenario. They were presenting it tomorrow. But Adam found it hard to care. He helped with the calculations. He helped write some of the scenes of horror that a roll of the dice would mean for each player, but he felt leaden, as if he weren't quite there. In some ways he felt numb, the way he read that some of the survivors of the bomb in Hiroshima had acted: 'Like walking ghosts, they didn't look like people of this world,' wrote one survivor.

It all seemed so strange to Adam. He knew that he had started to think about stealing the chess computer before they had begun on the Dungeons and Dragons doomsday scenario, but now the two were mixed up in his mind. He somehow felt that he had stolen the machine because doomsday was so near, but he knew that wasn't right.

'Adam!' Tracey was talking to him.

'Huh!'

'I was talking about setting up the scenario for those people who survive three months. Most of them will get cancer. What do you want to do about it?'

'What can I do about it?' Adam asked.

'Well, I thought we should set the scene. A roll of the dice will determine which kind of cancer you're going to get.'

'Don't forget sunburn,' said Jesse, lifting his head out of one of their research books. 'Some scientists think an atomic bomb will knock the ozone layer out, so no one will be able to go outside for more than ten minutes at a time without practically dying of sunburn. We've got to get the sunburn in.'

'Good point,' said Tracey. 'Come on, Adam, you and Jesse and I have to do the three-month survivors.'

Adam shook his head. 'I can't work on this anymore,' he said. 'I have to baby-sit for Alison again this afternoon. I promised my folks.'

'Boy, do they ever take advantage of you,' said Tracey. 'What are you? Their slave? You have to baby-sit every day.'

Adam felt stung. In the first place, he had volunteered to baby-sit because he wanted to be alone with the Chess Challenger. 'My parents can't help it if they don't have as much money as you,' snapped Adam.

'Well, ex-cuuuuse me,' said Tracey, drawing out each

syllable.

Jesse looked embarrassed. 'Hey, why don't we work over at Adam's house? I can bring the books and we can finish up the scenario. We've got to be ready tomorrow.'

'I've got a tap-dance class,' said Tiffany.

'Well, the three of us could work on it,' said Jesse. 'You could look at what we did in the morning.'

'I'm not sure that Adam wants to work on it,' said Tracey. 'Maybe he thinks Dungeons and Dragons doomsday scenario isn't worth working on.' Tracey was talking as if Adam weren't standing there.

'No, I want to do my share,' said Adam. 'My parents think it's a terrific idea. We can work at my house all afternoon.' Adam felt scared. He didn't want Tracey and Jesse in the house with him. He was almost afraid that the machine would start talking while they were there. He could just hear its monotone voice saying, 'Knight to bishop three ... I was stolen. I am the machine that said "Steal me."'

'Look, Tiffany and I will finish the firestorm scenario,' said Jesse, 'and I'll meet you over there in an hour, how's that?'

'Maybe Adam doesn't want me,' said Tracey.

'Tracey, please, you know that's not true. I'm sorry I'm so out of it. It's just all this talk about death. I'm sick of it.'

'You'd be more sick of it if a bomb really dropped on us,' said Tracey.

'Enough about the bomb,' Adam almost screamed. 'There is more to life than the end of the world.'

Tracey burst out laughing, and Adam laughed with her. It felt so good to laugh. Their eyes met and they laughed even harder.

'Come on,' said Tracey. 'Let's go. The rest of the doomsday team can meet us at your house. Okay, Jesse? Tiffany?'

Jesse looked up from his book. 'Sure,' he muttered. 'I'll be there soon.'

Tracey and Adam walked outside. The snow was falling

in big, heavy snowflakes. Adam couldn't see Tracey's face. The hood of her down parka kept her face hidden. They walked side by side in silence. Adam felt strangely at peace. It felt good to be in the snow, not in school, not at home, just in the snow with Tracey. He didn't feel cold, and he wished they could keep walking forever.

All too soon they reached Adam's house. He took out his key and let them in. He shook the snow off his jacket and took off his boots.

'Where's Alison?' asked Tracey.

'She's in a car pool. Somebody's mother will drop her off here around four-thirty.'

Tracey hung her parka on the coatrack. She stood in the hall as if waiting for Adam to say something. Adam could tell that she was tense. He realised that she didn't feel comfortable with him.

'Do you want a Coke or anything to drink?' Adam asked.

'Thank you,' said Tracey in an ultra-polite voice. 'A Coke would be nice.'

'Tracey, please don't use that voice with me,' begged Adam. 'It gives me the creeps.'

'You're the one who's been a creep,' said Tracey. 'Ever since we started working on the doomsday scenario. And I don't buy it that it's just the bomb that's got you upset. I hated that crack about my parents' money. You know, I never think about money when I'm with you.'

Adam laughed. 'You don't have to. You've got all the money you could want. Look, Tracey, I'm sorry I made that crack, but you do know you've got more money than my parents do.'

'I know, but your parents are terrific. I wouldn't mind having a mom and dad like yours. They love kids and they love you. Who cares that much about money?'

Adam sighed. He knew that it was easy for Tracey to say she didn't care about money. She had more than enough.

Tracey twirled her hair about her index finger. 'It's hard for me to talk about money,' she said. 'At home, mom and dad won't talk about it ever. Do you hate me because I have money and you don't?'

'No,' said Adam. 'But I can't help thinking about it some of the time.'

Tracey nodded as if she understood. Adam was grateful that they seemed to be friends again. Tracey wandered upstairs into Adam's room, the way she often did when they were together.

'Want to play a game of chess while we're waiting?' Tracey asked. 'I've been playing with my chess computer, but it's not the same as playing against a real person.'

'I know,' said Adam. The words slipped out before he realised what he had said.

'Did you get a machine?' Tracey asked.

'No,' said Adam as quickly as he could. 'But I can imagine that it would be boring to play against a machine.' Adam felt sure that his voice was giving him away. It sounded nervous and quaky to him.

'No, it's not boring,' corrected Tracey. 'It's just not as much fun. But you come to think of the machine as a person. I get mad at mine.'

'Oh, I'm sure,' said Adam. 'I'm absolutely sure that a chess machine has its own personality. A monster.'

Tracey stared at Adam. 'What are you talking about?' she asked. 'You sound crazy.'

Adam looked at the floor. Suddenly he wanted Tracey to know what he had done. Telling his father the lie about stealing a candy bar had only made things worse. Maybe Tracey would be able to help Adam, help him figure out what to do.

While they were talking, Tracey went over to his closet where she knew he kept his chess set.

'I'll get it,' said Adam, but Tracey was already reaching for the top shelf of his closet. The Monopoly box was on top of his chessboard. 'Monopoly,' said Tracey, holding the box in her hand. 'I haven't played that in a long time.'

'Give me that,' said Adam tersely. 'We can't play with just two. It's no fun.'

'It is too fun. I've had some great two-people Monopoly

games,' said Tracey.

'Give it to me,' insisted Adam through clenched teeth. He tried to wrest the Monopoly box from Tracey. Tracey held on to it.

'Not so fast . . . what are you so jumpy about? Have you got something hidden in here? Dirty pictures?' Tracey was laughing.

She held the box over her head. 'It's heavy. It's much heavier than a Monopoly game. Maybe it's a big book of dirty pictures.'

'Tracey, stop clowning around!' shouted Adam.

'No, I know you've got something filthy hidden in here,' said Tracey. 'You wouldn't be mad if you weren't hiding something.'

Tracey opened the lid of the box. Adam felt as if every nightmare that he had ever had was coming true in slow motion. Forget that moments ago he was thinking of telling Tracey himself. Then he had a choice; now all choice was being taken from him.

Tracey stared down at the box. She looked up. 'You've got a chess computer in here,' she said, as if perhaps Adam didn't know about it.

'I know,' said Adam, feeling like he had been struck dumb, as if someone had physically hit him in the stomach.

'You just said you didn't have a chess computer,' said Tracey, sounding terribly confused. 'What is this? One you stole?' Her voice cracked. Adam knew she was trying to be funny. What she didn't know was that she had hit upon the truth.

CHAPTER 18

CONFESSION

Adam took the box from Tracey's slack hands. He could tell Tracey wanted to hear some easy answer about where the computer came from. She looked as if she were almost pleading with him to explain it in a way that would make it all seem fine.

But Adam didn't want to tell another lie about the chess computer. He knew that he couldn't tell his parents the truth, but maybe he could tell Tracey.

'Sit down,' he said.

Tracey giggled. 'Is this where I hear your confession?' Her giggle sounded nervous.

Adam nodded. 'Will you?'

'Huh?'

'Hear my confession.'

'Adam, you've gone bonkers.'

'I know. Tracey, I stole that machine.'

Tracey's eyes opened wide. 'You stole it,' she repeated dumbly.

Adam paced around the room. He knew that even now he could make a joke about it. He could get out of telling the truth. Tracey didn't want to hear the truth. Maybe it wasn't fair to tell her about it. On the other hand, Adam felt so scared and confused himself that he had to tell somebody.

'Tracey, please listen to me. It's important.'

Tracey jumped off the bed. She, too, started pacing around the room. She looked down at the Chess Challenger. 'You stole it! It's worth a lot of money.'

'I know. It's been driving me crazy ever since I did it.'

'How did you ever get the nerve?' asked Tracey.

Adam stopped, stunned by her question. He had never thought of it as nerve. Wasn't she going to tell him how terrible he was?

'I don't know how I got the nerve. I invented a really complicated plot. First I stole a clock radio that also takes a cassette. Then I made a tape of a holdup note, only I didn't use my own voice. I told the saleslady to lock herself in the bathroom if she didn't want to get hurt. But they can't trace my voice. I got strangers in the mall to each say one word. No one knew what the whole sentence would be ...' As Adam spoke, he watched Tracey. She stared at him, blinking with every phrase. To Adam, his words sounded ridiculous, like a lunatic. He couldn't believe that he had actually gone to such trouble to steal something that he now hated. He hated the fact that he was a thief. The chess computer seemed like a lousy toy in comparison to the way he had felt before he stole it!

'I don't understand,' said Tracey. 'I thought you just stole the chess computer. You stoke a clock radio, too?'

'No,' said Adam. 'I returned the clock radio and pretended that Alison had taken it. That was the best part of my plan, at least that's what I first thought. The saleslady, Vanessa, thought I was a wonderful kid. Then I set the clock radio to go off the next afternoon. We had just started working on the doomsday scenario. I walked out of our doomsday and into the empty store. I took it.' With each word that Adam said his plan sounded crazier to him.

Tracey echoed his thought. 'That's the most stupid and complicated plan I've ever heard of. You're nuts. It's just like one of your chess moves or the way you sometimes play Dungeons and Dragons. You make such complicated strategy that a simple strategy can beat you.'

'Come on,' said Adam. 'Stop making such a big thing about it. Lots of kids steal things. And it worked, didn't it?'

'Sure it worked. But I don't steal,' said Tracey angrily. 'And I didn't think you were like lots of kids.' Adam realised that he didn't like to think of himself as just one of many kids who stole. He wished that he could go back and be like Tracey, someone who knew they had never stolen anything.

'I haven't enjoyed playing with the machine,' said Adam.

'Great,' said Tracey. 'I'm sure the judge will be very happy to hear that you haven't enjoyed it.'

'Are you going to turn me in?'

'No,' said Tracey. 'I wouldn't do that. But I bet they trace it to you. You pulled that idiotic theft of the clock radio, and you called attention to yourself.'

'She didn't know my name,' said Adam. 'You were the one who called me Sebastian when we went in there.'

Tracey fingered the chess pieces on the machine. 'What are you going to do with it? Are you going to keep it?'

'It gives me nightmares,' admitted Adam.

Just then, the doorbell rang. 'Jesse!' whispered Adam in a horrified voice. 'Jesse,' he repeated.

Tracey still had the Chess Challenger on her lap. 'Do you want me to hide it?' she asked.

Adam looked into her eyes. He wanted so much for her to respect and like him again. He thought about the lie that he told Jesse. In some way it had all started with that lie. Adam sighed deeply.

'No, Jesse's my friend. I'm going to tell him. And then somehow I'm going to take the machine back. It's not fair for me to always have secrets from Jesse.'

'But what if Jesse tells someone?' asked Tracey.

Adam shook his head. 'I've got to tell him, Tracey. We can't just pretend to work on the doomsday scenario as if nothing's happened.'

The doorbell rang again.

'Adam, I hope you know what you're doing,' said Tracey.

'I don't,' said Adam. He went to get the door.

Jesse stood on the front porch with a green garbage bag in his hand. 'It's freezing out here. What took you so long?'

'Come on in,' said Adam. 'I've got to talk to you.'

'What's wrong?' asked Jesse. 'You look as if you just found out doomsday is here.'

'It's got nothing to do with the atomic bomb or the end of the world,' said Adam. 'I've got a confession to make.'

Jesse flashed Adam a warning look. He grabbed Adam by the upper arm so tightly that his hands felt like a vice. 'If you told Tracey about me wetting my bed, I'll kill you,' hissed Jesse.

Adam shook his arm free. 'No, it's me who's got to confess.'

Meanwhile Tracey was trying frantically to get Adam's attention. 'Excuse me, Jesse,' she said. 'Adam, help me in the kitchen. I broke something.'

Adam followed her into the kitchen. 'What did you break?' he asked, wondering how Tracey had found time to go into the kitchen and break anything.

'Nothing,' said Tracey. 'It's just that the more I thought about it, the more I think you're crazy to tell Jesse.'

'Tracey,' said Adam, 'this is one thing you've got to let me decide. I've got to tell him.' Adam knew that somehow he had to tell Jesse the truth.

Adam went back out to the living room. Jesse stood in the middle, still looking worried that Adam was going to tell his secret.

Adam wished that he could reassure him. He felt that he owed Jesse something for the lie he had told him. He had learned the truth about Jesse. Jesse deserved to know the truth about him.

'Tracey found out that I stole a chess computer,' Adam blurted out almost all in one breath.

Jesse whistled. 'Geez, you've got a thing for computers, don't you? You're a repeater.'

'No,' said Adam angrily. 'I'm not. I lied to you the other night. I've never stolen anything before.'

'What are you guys talking about?' demanded Tracey.

'Nothing,' said Adam. 'At least nothing important. But I need your help. I want to get the machine back into the store without anyone knowing I took it.'

'Why?' asked Jesse.

Adam stared at him. *'Why?'*

'Yeah, why? As long as you stole it and got away with it, why risk taking it back?'

'Because I hate being a thief,' said Adam. 'Once I get it back to the store, I'll never steal again.'

'How do you know?' asked Tracey.

'I know. You didn't live through the last week. It wasn't worth it.'

Tracey looked as if she didn't believe Adam.

'I mean it,' said Adam.

'You don't have to convince me,' said Tracey.

'Come on, Tracey,' said Jesse. 'We've got to help Adam. Let's figure out a plan. It's sort of fun. It's like a Dungeons and Dragons scenario in reverse. Instead of finding the treasure, we've got to find a way to put it back.'

'It's not like a Dungeons and Dragons scenario or a chess game,' sighed Adam. 'That's what got me started in the first place. It's a real machine up there.'

'Let's see it,' said Jesse.

Adam brought it down. The magnetic chess pieces wobbled as he carried it down the stairs. Adam put it on the coffee table.

'It's small,' said Jesse. 'It's smaller than mine.'

'It's more expensive, too,' said Adam. 'Because it talks.'

'So how are you going to sneak it back into the store?' asked Jesse.

'You could just go in and confess,' said Tracey. 'You've confessed to me and you've confessed to Jesse. Why not just tell the truth?'

Adam realised he was sick of scheming. He didn't want a complicated plan. Tracey's words sounded so right.

CHAPTER 19

YOU'RE A REAL WEIRDO

At four-thirty, Alison was dropped off by her car pool. She looked like a toy spaceperson all wrapped up in her purple snowsuit. 'Don't bother to take it off,' said Adam. 'We're going to the mall.'

'Hi, Alison,' said Tracey, bending down so that she was at Alison's height. 'Do you want to go for a walk?'

Alison looked up at Adam as if she were confused by all the activity. She pouted. 'Juice,' she said.

'I'll get you a juice at the mall. Juice and a bagel,' said Adam, picking up Alison and putting her in her stroller.

'Poor kid, she doesn't even get a chance to pee,' said Tracey.

'They always change her diaper right before they put her in her snowsuit at day-care,' he said. 'She'll be okay.' He paused. 'She'll be okay if I don't end up in jail. If I do, will you bring her home?'

'You sound like a condemned man,' said Tracey.

'I feel like one,' said Adam.

They went outside. The temperature had dropped, and Adam felt chilled. He walked fast, rehearsing what he was going to say to Vanessa: 'I took this machine. I'm sorry, and I want to return it.'

'I don't think you should confess,' said Jesse. 'She'll probably call the police and call your parents. Why don't we just create a diversion and then you can slip the machine back.'

Adam was sweating even though it was cold outside. 'I can't do it that way,' he said.

Tracey said nothing. She wheeled Alison's stroller along the narrow, shovelled path.

'What do you think?' Adam asked her.

'I don't know. You seem to have this need to confess.'

'Well, what would you do?' demanded Adam.

'Yeah,' said Jesse. 'You might steal sometime. Rich kids steal, too. Haven't you ever stolen anything?'

Tracey shook her head.

'I have,' said Jesse. 'I stole a Rubik's Cube, and I didn't return it.'

They reached the mall. Tracey went in first. The computer store's sign shone in the weird, yellowish light of the mall. Adam's legs felt like Jell-O. 'Are you really going to tell her?' Tracey whispered. 'We don't have to. We can do it Jesse's way and just sneak it back if you want.'

Adam felt torn. He didn't *want* to tell Vanessa what he had done. He was scared to death that she would call the police. But it didn't feel right to just sneak the machine back. After all, he was the one who made the tape that frightened her into locking herself in the bathroom.

'Too bad you can't just tape your confession and leave it,' said Jesse.

Adam wished he could do that. Alison chose that moment to wake up from a sound sleep. *'Bagel!'* she shouted, smelling the hot bagels from the bagel shop.

'I'll get her one,' said Tracey.

'I'll go with you,' said Jesse.

Adam realised that his friends didn't want to have to watch him confess. 'Okay,' said Adam. 'I'll meet you out here. I did it myself. I'd better finish it myself.'

He looked into the computer store. Behind the banks of consoles, Vanessa was talking to a customer. She saw

Adam and gave him a friendly wave.

Adam looked around for Jesse and Tracey. He realised that he couldn't just confess. He felt like he was choking. He walked into the computer store.

Vanessa was typing something into the keyboard to show the customer.

Adam stared at her back. He felt as if his heart were beating somewhere in the middle of his throat. How could he interrupt her and tell her he was a thief? He couldn't stand it. Suppose she did call the police? He would be branded as a thief all his life.

Suddenly, Adam knew that he didn't have the nerve to confess. He felt the weight of the Chess Challenger in his knapsack. He kept his eye on Vanessa. She still had her back to him. He bent down and slipped the Chess Challenger out of the knapsack. He stuck it on a low shelf.

Then he stood up. Vanessa turned around and smiled at him. 'I'll be with you in a minute,' she said.

'I'll be back,' Adam muttered. 'I forgot something outside.'

Adam tried to walk normally to the door. He felt a hundred pounds lighter. The machine was returned, and he hadn't needed to confess.

He saw Jesse across the mall, wheeling an empty stroller.

'Where's Tracey and Alison?' Adam asked.

'Alison insisted on getting out of her stroller, and Tracey decided you needed her moral support. She went to find you in the computer store. There they are.' Jesse pointed to the computer store. Through the plate glass, Adam could see Tracey and Alison looking for him.

'Did you confess?' Jesse asked.

'I couldn't,' said Adam. 'Let's get Tracey and Alison out of the shop and get out of here. I want to go home.'

They headed for the computer store. As they were walking in, the customer was walking out. Adam started for Tracey and Alison when suddenly he heard a high-pitched voice say, 'Oh, Adam's game!'

Adam froze. The store seemed absolutely silent. Then to Adam's horror, he heard the sound of the voice of the Chess Challenger. 'Queen to knight five!' Alison waved the chess piece in the air.

Tracey tried to wrestle the chess piece out of Alison's hand. Adam's feet felt as if they had grown roots. He saw Vanessa glare at Tracey.

'*My God*, it's the stolen machine!' shouted Vanessa. Tracey looked desperately at Adam. Vanessa grabbed Tracey by the arms. 'You!' said Vanessa. 'You've been in here so much. You must have been the one who planted that ridiculous tape. What are you doing here? Trying to steal something else?'

Tracey shook her head, but she was unable to speak. Meanwhile Alison was taking each chess piece off the machine, causing the machine to go berserk as it tried to keep up with all the mvoes. 'Knight to Queen three. Beep. Bishop to King five.' Every time Alison lifted a piece, the machine responded.

'*Well, young lady.* Do you have anything to say for yourself?' demanded Vanessa.

'*She didn't take it!*' shouted Adam. His voice was so loud that Alison stopped picking up the chess pieces. She toddled over to Adam and gave him the chess piece in her hand. Adam looked down at it. Alison had captured the black knight.

He bent down and picked up the pieces that Alison had scattered all over the store. He stood up and faced Vanessa.

'I stole the chess computer,' he said. 'I brought it back today because I hated myself for stealing it. But Tracey didn't have anything to do with it.'

'You're the kid who stole the clock radio and brought it back,' said Vanessa. 'You put in that crazy tape. What are you, some kind of perverted kid who gets his kicks out of stealing things and then bringing them back?'

'No ...' stammered Adam.

Vanessa was so angry she was shaking. '*Get out of here. All of you. You're nuts, do you know that?* If you ever step

107

foot in this store again, I'll call the cops. I'd call them right now, but they'd never believe this story. You're a real weirdo.'

Of all the things that Adam had expected to happen when he confessed, he never imagined Vanessa kicking him out of the store.

He backed out of the store. Tracey scooped Alison up into her arms and followed him. Jesse trailed after them, bringing the stroller.

They retreated to the fountain in the middle of the mall. Jesse couldn't stop giggling nervously.

'It's not funny,' insisted Adam. 'She really thinks I'm nuts.'

'She terrified me,' said Tracey. 'And she really hates you.'

'I know,' said Adam.

'But it was crazy in there,' said Jesse. 'It was like a scene from a movie.'

'It was *not*!' said Adam. 'It wasn't like a movie. I still feel creepy.'

Jesse said, 'Come on, we'd better get out of here.'

Adam nodded. 'You know, our doomsday presentation tomorrow is going to seem like a pleasure compared to today.'

As they left the mall, Adam stole one last look at the computer store. He thought about the fact that he could never go in there again. Vanessa had seemed like such a nice woman, and she hated him. She would always think of him as a crazy kid who couldn't be trusted.

CHAPTER 20

SURVIVOR

Adam returned to an empty house. Neither Tracey nor
Jesse had wanted to come home with him, causing Adam
to wonder if each had made an excuse to get away from
him. Once the computer was returned, they all seemed to
experience a peculiar let-down feeling. They had split up
at the mall, and Adam had taken Alison home. With each
step, he had been aware that the incriminating evidence
was gone. He could feel adrenaline rushing through him,
almost as strong as the day that he stole the computer. It
made him feel skittish, as if once again his heart was
beating too fast and was too big for his body. The relief
was immense, and yet, Adam felt as if something wasn't
finished. He wished that Tracey and Jesse hadn't left him
alone. He needed to talk to them, to find out what they
thought.

He got Alison out of her snowsuit and put her upstairs
for a nap. He knew his parents would be home soon. He
paced around his room, trying to go over his part for the
doomsday presentation. The words blurred together. He
couldn't concentrate. He felt as if his mind were a separate
being, no longer under his control. He kept hearing
Vanessa screaming at him. The memory of her voice sent

flashes of shame pumping through his body. Adam paused in front of the telephone. Quickly he picked up the receiver and dialled Tracey's private number. She had her own telephone number, a different one from her parents'. She picked it up on the first ring.

'Tracey, it's me, Adam.'

She laughed nervously. 'It must be ESP. I was going to call you. I just had my hand on the telephone. You didn't look so good when we left you at the mall. I was going to call to see if you were all right.'

Adam felt his body relax just at the sound of Tracey's voice.

'Adam, are you okay?'

'Fine ... I was ... No, I'm not fine. I feel strange. I don't know. I thought maybe you and Jesse hated me or something.'

'You're nuts,' said Tracey. 'Whoops, I didn't mean to say that. I know the woman in the store called you nuts, but you know what I mean. Why would Jesse and I hate you? We helped you, didn't we?'

'I don't know. I thought maybe you were mad because I got you involved in such a crazy thing.'

'It did feel crazy,' said Tracey. 'But it was worse when you were acting so strange, and we didn't know why. Besides, it's over now. The computer is back. You got away with it.'

'I know, but ...'

'Listen, Adam, stop thinking about it. It's over. If you want to worry about something, worry about our doomsday presentation. I'm scared about it. What if we bomb?'

Adam laughed. 'If we bomb, it'll just remind everyone about doomsday, get it?'

'Very funny. Anyhow, forget about the chess computer. If you want to take your mind off it, just think about doomsday.'

'I'm trying, but suppose doomsday doesn't come.'

'Huh? What are you talking about?'

'When I stole the chess computer, I told myself I deserved it because the world might end at any moment. But then the world didn't end. I was stuck with the chess computer and feeling lousy. I was scared because I had stolen something so expensive. Do you understand?'

'Sort of,' said Tracey, but she sounded unsure. 'Look, I've got to go now. I'll see you early tomorrow at school. Remember, we're going to meet early for the final run-through?'

'Right,' said Adam, feeling as if he had tried to explain too much. He hung up. He felt a little better after talking to Tracey. Clearly, she didn't hate him. But still, he had a queer, unfinished feeling, as if the ghost of the chess computer was still haunting him.

The feeling was still with him the next morning as his parents drove him to school. His mother turned around to face Adam in the backseat. 'Are you nervous about your presentation?' she asked.

'Not very,' said Adam. 'I have to present the odds and give the statistics about how many people will be killed. In our game, you roll a dice to determine if you're killed or if you're a survivor.'

'It sounds like a hard job,' said his father.

Adam shrugged. 'You mean, 'cause I have to tell them that eventually there won't be any survivors?' He wished his voice hadn't gone up in a squeak.

His mother stared at him. 'You know, there's more to life than doomsday.'

Adam laughed. 'That's funny. Tracey and I have been telling each other the same thing for weeks.'

'Dad and I are proud of you for being so concerned, but we don't want you to think about nuclear war all the time. But you still have to go on enjoying life, loving life.' She laughed at herself. 'Now look who's giving lectures.' She glanced at Adam's father.

Adam's father reached over and squeezed her hand; a warm smile spread across his face. Adam felt in his gut how much they loved each other. But would they love him

111

if they knew the truth?

They turned into the driveway of the school. The landscape looked bleak, like a black-and-white photograph. Suddenly, Adam longed for the colour of winter in California, the green from the rain, the burnt amber of the hills, the bold, bright, red and pink tropical flowers. His parents parked the car. 'We'll see you at the assembly,' said his father. Adam nodded absently.

He went into school and down to the Math-Science Club. The others were already there. 'I'm nervous,' said Tracey as a greeting. 'I could hardly sleep last night.'

'I never think of you as nervous,' said Tiffany.

'Think again,' said Tracey. 'Somehow I feel even more nervous than when we're doing a class play.'

'That's because this time we wrote the play,' said Adam.

'You're right,' agreed Tracey. 'Well, it's too late to back out now. My parents took the day off to come to the assembly.'

'Mine, too,' said Jesse. 'Both my mom and my dad came. I called my dad and told him I wanted him to be here.'

'Your parents are coming, Adam, aren't they?' asked Tiffany. 'After all, they're here already.'

Adam resented her question. She sounded as if she didn't think his parents did real work. 'Yeah, Dad got the other first-grade teacher to take his class for the hour. Mom is closing the library.'

'I think we should make sure all the adults play, too,' said Tracey. 'Let them roll the dice and start the maze. It will be good to have some adult casualties and adult survivors.'

'Yeah, but nobody survives for long,' said Jesse. He sounded so excited about the prospect. Adam felt tired. He wished the assembly was over. He was glad that it was scheduled for the first period.

They took the maps and mazes up to the assembly hall. They had enough copies so that everyone would get a maze, and they put copies on each seat. Then they went up on the stage to wait. As the fifth- and sixth-graders

112

marched in, Adam could see several kids giggle as they looked at the doomsday maze on their seats.

'Welcome to the Doomsday Dungeons and Dragons game,' said Tracey when everyone had quietened down. 'I know that several of you have heard about our game, but we wanted a chance to share it with all of you. It isn't really a game. We wanted to show exactly how horrible nuclear war will be. Some politicians and generals think that we can survive a nuclear war. Our game will show you what survival will be like. Some of you will roll a dice and be killed instantly. You will be the lucky ones. Others will survive for a few hours, days, weeks, or even months. But you will face cancer from radiation, famine because no food will grow, and horrible plagues because of diseases spread by dying bodies. We think that by playing by the rules of a Dungeons and Dragons game we can bring the horror home. The people who control nuclear weapons are like kids playing Dungeons and Dragons. They don't think the roll of the dice is real. We do.'

Adam looked out over the audience. His parents were staring at him, with a proud half-smile on their lips. His mother began to clap and soon everyone joined in. To Adam's surprise, tears were in his eyes. He felt embarrassed to be crying, but more than anything in the world he wanted to return to being the kid his parents thought he was.

Adam could barely remember his speech. From his notes, he read the statistics for survival. He got a round of applause, but it sounded weak compared to the ovation Tracey had received. Then, finally, the presentation was over. They came down from the stage while the teachers arranged everyone into small groups so that they could play a sample game.

Adam's parents made their way through the crowd. His mother hugged him. 'You were wonderful. We want to play in your game. Is that all right?'

'Sure,' said Adam as his father game him a hug. 'Everyone is talking about how terrific you were,' he whispered.

'Thanks,' Adam muttered.

His father picked up the multi-sided dice. 'Now to see how I end up.' He rolled it in his palm for several seconds. Then he let the dice fall.

Adam stared at it. 'Number three. You're dead. The bomb vapourised your body and nothing is left. You're floating in air, just radioactive dust.'

'I hope I don't poison you,' Adam's father handed the dice to his wife. 'I hope I die quickly, too,' she said as she rolled the dice.

'Number nine. You're in an outlying area,' said Adam. 'A building falls on you and crushes your legs, but it takes you hours to die. I'm sorry, Mom.'

'It's not your fault,' said his mother. She handed him the dice. 'Your turn.'

Adam rolled it in his hand, conscious as he did so that he was imitating his father. He threw the dice down on the table.

'Eighteen,' said his father. 'Does that make you a survivor?'

Adam nodded. 'I survive for four months. Four long months. I have to watch you die, and then I get radiation sickness, and I die, too.' He walked away, suddenly feeling closed in by all the people. His parents followed him. 'Adam, are you okay?' asked his father.

'I just need a little air.'

'Let's *all* get some air,' said his father.

'Just let me get my jacket,' said his mother.

'No, no,' said Adam. 'I'm okay – really.'

'Come on,' said his father. 'You look as if you need a blast of cold Buffalo air. It'll clear the doomsday radiation right out of your system. And the others can play this game without you.'

Adam got his jacket and met his parents at the front door. They stood close together under the giant stone archway, dwarfed by the Gothic proportions of the school. Adam's mother reached out her hand to Adam. They walked down the shovelled path. Adam breathed deep. The air did feel good, and he felt privileged that his parents worked here, that they could take a walk together in the middle of the day. The sun was out, making it almost too dazzling to look at the snow. 'It's beautiful out now, isn't it?' said Adam's mother. She swung his hand gently the way she used to when he was very young.

'Dad and I have been talking,' she said. 'We know things haven't been easy since we moved back to Buffalo. We want you to know we couldn't have survived if you hadn't been such a terrific, level-headed kid. We love you a lot, and I'm glad you're a survivor in more ways than one.'

'Mom, stop it.'

'No, I mean it, Adam, you're just a terrific kid.'

Adam dropped his mother's hand. 'Mom, cut it out!' he cried.

His father caught the change in his tone of voice. 'What's going on? I get the feeling something is really bothering you.'

'He's just been contemplating the end of the world,' said his mother. 'Isn't that enough?'

'I mean something personal.'

'It's not our business to pry.'

Adam listened, wondering whether he had the nerve to tell them the truth. What would they say if they knew? Adam swallowed. They would think he was crazy!

'*Is* something bothering you?' asked his father.

'Sure,' said Adam. He tried to laugh. 'Lots of things bother me. I wish we had more money. I wish ...'

'Oh, Adam.' His mother sighed. 'You can't wish for money just to *buy* things. There will always be something else you want that costs more money than you have. Someday you have to stop thinking that *things* are so important.'

Adam felt anger rise within him like a tornado. 'Well, I wanted a chess computer so much, I didn't just wish for it. I stole it! There, that's how much your perfect little boy wanted something!'

Adam turned and ran away down the path. His father grabbed him by the arm. '*Adam!* What did you say?'

'You heard me!' He wasn't sure where he wanted to run to, but he wanted to get far away, far away from the school and far from his parents.

His mother caught up with them. 'Did he say he stole a chess computer?'

Adam gasped for breath. His father's grip on his forearm tightened. 'Let's get into the car,' he said. 'Let's talk about this out of the cold and in private.'

They took off across the lawn of pristine snow. Adam heard the snow crunch as he walked. He wished it would open up and swallow him. His father opened the car door. Adam got in between his parents in the front seat. He stared out the windshield.

'Adam, please tell us again what you did,' asked his father in a voice so full of bewilderment that Adam felt sorry for him.

'You don't have to worry,' said Adam. 'I returned the machine yesterday. Nobody knows I took it.'

'You returned it?' His father still sounded puzzled. 'Then you didn't steal it.' He turned to Adam's mother with relief. 'He didn't steal it.'

'I did, too,' said Adam. 'I stole it. Then I returned it.' He felt suspended between laughing and crying. His voice was high. He knew he sounded almost hysterical.

'Adam, tell us what happened from the beginning,' said his mother in a voice she used when she was trying to keep calm.

'I shouldn't have told you,' said Adam, shaking his head. 'I should have kept it a secret.'

'No, you shouldn't have kept it a secret,' snapped his mother. 'Now tell us what happened.'

Adam began his tale. He felt so foolish that he kept stumbling over his words. His parents listened to him in total silence. Adam wished they would say something, anything, to stop the flow of his words. And words weren't the only thing that were flowing. Tears streamed down his face, and his nose dripped, too. Finally, he reached the end. He told how Vanessa had kicked him out of the store, screaming at him, 'You're nuts, you know!'

His father shook his head. 'Adam, Adam ...'

'I know. You think I'm crazy, too.'

'You don't know what I think or how I feel about this!' shouted his father.

'Don't shout,' warned his mother.

'I'll shout if I want to! Listen to me, Adam, and listen good. I don't think you're crazy. I don't think that's an excuse. I think you felt sorry for yourself, and you did something incredibly stupid. But no, I don't think you're crazy.'

Adam sniffed and wiped his eyes. He felt silly, but he felt relieved to have his father yelling at him, telling him that he was not crazy.

'How could you steal!?' exclaimed his father. 'You seemed to be listening and understanding when I talked to you about how I felt about stealing. Were you laughing at me that night when I talked to you about trust?'

Adam felt stung by his father's words. 'No, I had already stolen the computer. I felt bad about it even then. I lied to you about the candy bar.'

His father sighed. 'Computer, candy bar, the principle is the same.'

'How can you say that?' exploded his mother. 'Adam said the computer cost four hundred dollars. That's more than my take-home pay for two weeks' work.' She sounded furious. 'I went to college and graduate school. I earned my own way. I help pay for our rent, our food, your clothes. Four hundred dollars is not something I *ever, ever* have just thrown away on a toy. Four hundred dollars!'

'Grace, now you're shouting!'

'Of course I'm shouting!'

Adam felt as if he were crumbling. His mother stopped. 'Adam ...' she said in a quieter voice. She couldn't seem to find the words to go on. Adam felt as if he had hurt her so badly.

'I'm sorry,' Adam said.

'I know you are,' she said. 'I can see it in your face, but ...'

'Are you going to punish me?' Adam asked.

His father sighed. 'Yeah, we're going to dock your allowance for the next twenty years so you can understand how much four hundred dollars is!' said his father sarcastically. 'Adam, I don't know what punishment to give you. You're obviously sorry, but it was so stupid. Sorry isn't enough. What would you have done if you had damaged the machine and had to pay back the four hundred dollars?'

'I would have worked for it or paid it back somehow,' said Adam, feeling very defensive.

'How, Adam? Think about it, for God's sake,' said his mother. 'How many hours would you have to baby-sit? Remember when you held the yard sale in California before we left? You sold off all your old toys and games. How much did you make?'

'Nearly thirty dollars,' answered Adam.

'So what do you think you could do to earn it if you had to pay back the four hundred dollars?' his father asked.

'I took the damn machine back!' yelled Adam. 'I did!'

'You were damn lucky, Adam,' snapped his father. 'Think of the consequences if you had been caught. You were lucky that woman at the computer store didn't call the police.'

'*I know! I know!*' screamed Adam. But he felt far from lucky. He felt scared that his parents were so disappointed in him. Adam, the good, perfect, funny, smart kid was now Adam the Terrible.

'Hey, let's all calm down,' said his mother. 'First of all you came and told us. That's a good thing. Secondly, you aren't going to jail. That's another good thing. Thirdly, you obviously decided yourself that you didn't like being a thief. That took guts.'

'Fifth of all, it's not the end of the world,' added Adam's father, trying to make a feeble joke.

'That's fourth of all,' said Adam. 'I kept count.' His mother laughed nervously. Adam blinked his eyes. 'When you were a kid, did you ever do anything like this? I mean, steal.'

His mother looked embarrassed. She squirmed in the car seat, and then brushed her hair away from her face. 'Well, I never told your dad about this, but I once stole a book from a bookstore. It was a stupid bookstore to steal from. The store had a balcony running around the second floor. They had detectives up there looking down at the customers. I got caught right away. It was the most humiliating experience I ever had. I begged the detectives not to call my parents.'

'How old were you?' Adam asked. It seemed incredible to imagine his mother stealing a book and begging a detective not to call her parents.

'I was seventeen. Old enough to know better.' She smiled. 'But so were you, old enough to know better.'

'I know,' said Adam. 'I'm never going to do it again. I can promise you that.'

'I believe you,' said his mother. The windshield of the car was completely clouded over from their breath.

'We've got to get back to class,' said his father. 'Adam, you've got to get back, too. I'm glad you talked to us about this. We'll talk more about it later.'

'Okay,' said Adam. They walked through the snow back to the huge stone mansion that housed the school. Adam's father rested his arm on Adam's shoulder without saying anything. His father's arm felt heavy, but Adam was glad it was there.

CHAPTER 21

A KID YOU CAN TRUST

'I can't come and play a real D and D game. And I can't stay overnight,' Adam told Jesse when he called that night. 'I'm being punished. I'm grounded. I told my parents about stealing the chess computer.'

'You told them! Why did you do that?' Jesse asked.

Adam wondered about it himself. But he knew he felt better. His parents had been angry, but now they knew the worst. They might be mad, but they still loved him. In fact, they told him so often they loved him that Adam had to tell them to cut it out.

'I'm not sure why I told them.' It was hard to explain it to Jesse. 'I told them right after the doomsday present-ation. We went for a walk. They were going on and on about how proud they were of me. I couldn't stand it. I told them the truth.'

'Did they hit the ceiling?'

'We were outside. There was no ceiling, but, yeah, they were mad. My dad *hates* stealing. He says that it steals trust.'

'Well, my dad doesn't exactly love stealing. But it sounds like they came down real heavy. How long are you grounded for?'

'Two weeks. They're also docking my allowance. I'm supposed to learn to appreciate the value of a dollar.'

Jesse laughed. 'You're the tightest kid with a buck I know.'

'Well, I'll be a little tighter from now on.' When he hung up, Adam realised that for the first time he hadn't minded talking about money to Jesse. He went into the kitchen. The sun was streaming through the window. His parents were having a cup of coffee; classical music played softly in the background. With Alison up taking a nap, it was very preaceful.

'That was Jesse,' said Adam. 'He asked me to come over tonight, but I told him I was grounded.'

His mother sipped her coffee. 'Actually, Dad and I were just going to talk to you about tonight.'

'And tomorrow,' added his father quickly. Adam felt an anxious flutter in his stomach. As always, his mother seemed able to read his mind. 'Don't look that way. It's good news.'

'What is it?' asked Adam warily.

'Well, let's take tomorrow first,' said his father. 'Your mother has decided to take the plunge. She's going to try to get on a pair of skis. We're all going to the slopes tomorrow. You and I will teach her.'

His mother laughed. 'You don't have to sound as if this is the miracle of the century.'

'What about tonight?' Adam asked.

'We'll get to that. Aren't you pleased that we're going skiing tomorrow?'

'Great. Now what about tonight. Why do I get the feeling I'm not going to like it?'

'It's nothing terrible. It's just that tonight your mom and I are going over to the Vickers' for dinner. We asked Melanie Vickers to come over here and baby-sit.'

'I hate that!' said Adam angrily. 'I don't need a baby-sitter.'

'Hold it, Adam,' said his father. 'It's for Alison. We're not doing this to punish you.'

'Oh, sure!'

'Adam, sit down,' said his mother. 'Listen to us. This is not to punish you. But your dad and I have spent a lot of time talking about what happened.' She laughed nervously. 'Probably too much. I'm a little obsessed about it. I know you are a great kid. And I love you. We both love you. But somehow I think your stealing was a little bit our fault. We've put a lot of pressure on you to grow up. We gave you an awful lot of responsibility. I don't blame you for being angry at us.'

'I wasn't angry!' shouted Adam.

'I'm not so sure,' said his mother. 'Anyhow, we decided to try to take the pressure off you for a bit. We're not going to insist that you take care of Alison all the time.'

'Great! You say you're not punishing me. But I'm grounded! I can't go over to Jesse's for the night! Now I have to have a stupid baby-sitter!'

'Melanie is not stupid. She's in the ninth grade. And she's here to baby-sit for Alison. You can do whatever you want. You're grounded, but you can do your homework or watch television or read, all without having to worry about Alison. We thought you'd be relieved.'

'If I'm going to stay home, I'd rather baby-sit for Alison. Please call Melanie up and tell her she doesn't have to come.'

'No,' insisted his mother. 'We want to give this a try. I think it'll be good.'

'It's no good,' said Adam. But he knew his parents. He knew that once they'd made up their minds, they wouldn't change them.

'I'm not going to talk to her,' warned Adam.

'Come on, Adam,' said his father. 'I wish you wouldn't take it like this.'

'Well, there's nothing you can do about how I take it, is there?' Adam snapped.

'No, there isn't,' admitted his mother.

Adam was still angry that evening when Melanie Vickers

came to the door. Adam had seen her around school. She was short and just a little pudgy, but she had the biggest boobs in the ninth grade. Adam could imagine the jokes Jesse would make if he found out she had baby-sat for him. He hoped Jesse would never find out.

'Hi, Adam,' said Melanie. 'I'm here to baby-sit for Alison.'

Adam figured his parents had coached her. 'Come on in, Melanie' said his mother. 'You're lucky. Alison's already in bed and quiet. I'll go over the routine for you if she wakes up.'

'I have to go upstairs. I've got a lot of homework,' said Adam coldly.

His mother looked at him. 'Good night, Adam.' She tried to give him a kiss. 'Get plenty of rest. You're going to need a lot of strength to pull your mom out of snowbanks tomorrow.'

Adam recognised her hearty voice. He knew she was trying to be nice, but he was still mad. He went up to his room and closed the door. He heard his father shout good night, and then the sound of their car pulling out of the driveway. He heard Melanie turn on the television set. Adam wondered what to do with himself. He didn't have much homework, and he didn't feel like reading. 'It would be a perfect time to play with a chess computer,' he thought. But he was only kidding himself. He was glad the computer was out of his life.

However, he absolutely hated having a baby-sitter in the house. Adam thought about skiing the next day. His parents thought they were giving him such a treat. Well, tomorrow Adam would tell them again what he thought – a baby-sitter was punishment.

He'd tell them that it felt creepy having someone else take over his job.

He'd tell them it was embarrassing.

He'd tell them that he didn't like having a ninth-grade girl do something that he had done well.

He'd make them understand that he was a kid they could

trust. Adam was in the middle of an imaginary conversation with his parents when he heard a knock on his door. Melanie stood in the doorway. 'What are you doing?' she asked.

'Not much.'

'I hear you're a great chess player. Do you want to play a game?'

Adam hesitated. He wanted his parents to know how much he was suffering with a baby-sitter around, but on the other hand, he was bored. He realised he didn't want to sulk in his room all night. He followed Melanie downstairs and showed her where they kept the chess set.

To Adam's surprise, she was a good player. The evening went by quickly. She beat him in the first game, and then he fought her to a draw. In the final game, Adam thought he was winning, but his parents came home before they could finish.

'Well, I see you have something in common,' said Adam's father. Adam regretted that his parents had come home while they were still playing. Now they'd think that he liked having Melanie baby-sit. 'Come on, Melanie,' said his father. 'I'll take you home. Perhaps you and Adam can finish the game another time.'

'I'll concede,' said Melanie. 'I think Adam would have won anyhow.'

Adam put away the chess set as his mother watched. She took off her shoes and sank into the sofa, her legs crossed under her. 'It looks like you and Melanie had a pretty good time tonight,' she said.

Adam felt angry all over again. His parents thought everything was just fine!

'I think you should go to bed,' said his mother. 'We have a big day tomorrow.'

Suddenly Adam couldn't wait until morning. 'There's something I've got to talk to you about,' he said.

His mother laughed. 'I have a friend who says that those are the most frightening words in the English language.'

'This is serious, Mom.'

'I'm sorry. What is it?'

'Can we wait till Dad gets back? I want to talk to both of you.'

'Adam, it's late.'

'This is serious.' Just then the car pulled into the driveway. Adam's father walked in. 'How come you two aren't upstairs?' he asked.

'Adam wants to talk to us. But I'm warning you, Adam, we're all tired.'

Adam resented that she was making it so hard for him to say what he wanted to say. He knew he had to tell them why he was angry. 'I really hated having Melanie baby-sit.'

'Not that again,' groaned his father. 'You looked like you were having a pretty nice time. Melanie said you were good company and a fine chess player.'

Adam sighed. When he prepared the speech in his head, it had been much easier.

'Can't this wait until tomorrow?' his father asked.

'No, it can't,' insisted Adam. Then he stopped short. He couldn't think of what to say next. It was as if his long list had flown from his memory, as if a computer's memory bank had blown.

'Well, what is it?' Adam could see his father was tired. His mother brushed her hair away nervously. She looked at Adam inquisitively.

'I . . . I . . . I felt like you don't trust me anymore.' Adam knew that of all the items on his list, this was the only one that counted.

His parents glanced at each other. 'What do you mean?' his mother asked.

'I trusted you,' said Adam. 'I told you the truth about stealing. And look what you turned around and did. I didn't mind being grounded. That was real punishment. But making me have a baby-sitter was sneaky!'

'Adam, wait a minute,' said his father. 'We told you it wasn't part of your punishment.'

'You're lying,' said Adam flatly. 'You don't trust me with Alison anymore.'

125

'Hold it a minute,' said his mother. 'We're not lying.'

'You are,' insisted Adam. 'You got a baby-sitter because you don't trust me.' Adam's mother lowered her eyes. Adam wanted her to deny it. Instead she sighed. 'I'm right, aren't I?' asked Adam defiantly.

Adam's mother shook her head. 'No, we didn't lie to you. We told you the truth. But it's complicated. Maybe there was more to it than we thought. I certainly didn't realise it would upset you like this.' She looked across at Adam's father. 'He could be right. Maybe we did have a hidden agenda.'

His father rubbed his beard. 'Look, Adam, we didn't mean to hurt you. I know that might not seem like much of an apology to you. You didn't mean to hurt us when you stole the chess computer, either. But it did hurt. Maybe we didn't think it all the way through. We make mistakes, too. But you've got to understand. You gave us a shock. We can't just turn around on a dime.'

'So you *are* punishing me?' Adam didn't feel particularly triumphant to learn that he was right.

His mother shook her head. 'No, that's not what your father is trying to say. Honestly, we didn't mean to punish you. But I think you're right, we didn't realise how much it would hurt you. I'm sorry.'

'Trust isn't something you can tear down and build up at will,' said his father. 'It takes work on both sides.'

'I want you to trust me again,' said Adam.

'You're proving it,' said his father. 'Just tonight, by talking to us like this. You know, Adam, you might have done a stupid thing, but you are a kid you can trust – and love.'

Adam swallowed hard. 'I hated thinking that you didn't trust me.'

'Let's go to bed,' said his father. 'We still have a day of skiing ahead of us.' He gave Adam a hug. Adam hugged him back. 'A kid you can trust.' Adam liked the sound of those words. Now he would have to live up to them.